ENDANGERED

By

Claire Rye

In the grand fresco of existence, humans held the brush that painted their destiny.
Alas, they chose strokes of negligence and shortsightedness, and in their own masterpiece, they became the architects of their extinction.
Anonymous circa 2023

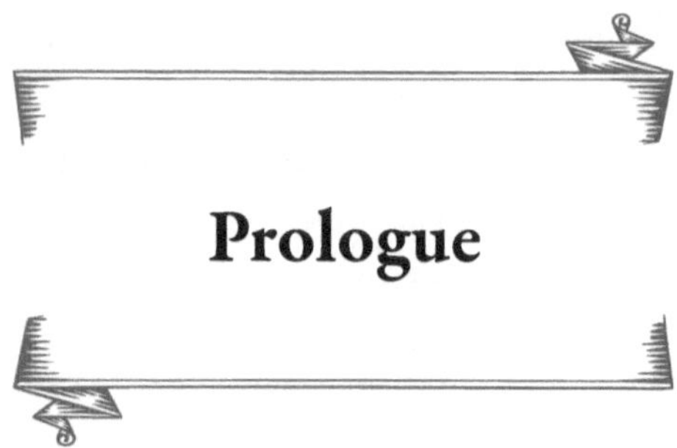

Prologue

Jenny strained to open her eyes. The exhaustion was full body now and she could barely find consciousness through her dark thoughts. Her eyes opened enough for a small slither of light to draw her out of her sleep. She blinked a few times, her dry eyes stinging from the movement of her lids. She didn't complain, Jenny never complained.

She looked down at her forearm, her pale skin was covered with Goosebumps. She was obviously cold, but as she looked at her uncovered arm, it occurred to her she didn't feel the sensation of being chilled. Jenny now felt nothing, not even numb.

"Josh," she whispered, "are you cold?" she turned her head slowly to look at the young man lying beside her. "Josh?"

He looked so peaceful. Like a baby sleeping, without a care in the world. She smiled at the man she had met seven weeks before. He was funny and charming and had made the endless hours on the steel bench almost bearable. Almost.

Josh was better company than the woman who occupied his spot before him. She screamed and cried on and off for days. Yelling for help like it would have made a difference. Jenny tried to comfort her, tried to offer reason, support. It was useless. The woman before Josh wanted two things that this place would never give her. Hope and freedom.

Josh was more like Jenny. Despite the unchangeable situation, they both made the best out of it. Connecting with those around them and talking people through the process of acceptance.

Before they met, before they were captured, Jenny and Joshua were of the same nature - optimistic and kind, and they saw no sense in changing, especially now when their compassion was needed the most.

"Jooosh!" Jenny called softly. "Wake up, I'm bored." she paused and waited for a response.

Normally, he would make a joke about being busy or having other plans, but today he was silent.

"Joshua, don't make me come over there," she jested. Hoping humour might tease out a response.

Jenny stared at Joshua's naked body. A body that although she had never touched, she knew every inch of. His once muscular thickset build had been reduced to a scrawnier, gaunt shell of a man. She focused on his chest. The lush masculine hair scarcely disguising the bony frame beneath. Despite the deterioration, she still found him attractive.

Jenny watched his motionless body, waiting for any movement. She swallowed hard as she realised the rise and fall of his chest had stopped. She waited. Maybe he would exhale? Maybe his breathing was shallow? Maybe he was playing a joke?

She waited, but there was no change.

Jenny knew where she could find confirmation, but she couldn't muster the courage to look.

She closed her eyes and squeezed out a tear from her dehydrated ducts. Her chin trembling from the thought of knowing he was gone. She composed herself and bravely opened her eyes, looking straight at Joshua's wrist. The iron clamp that held the cannula in place was flashing red, a sure sign the body had run out of blood. The intravenous tube was empty, and the machine designed to suck the humans dry read - 'new source required.'

Joshua was dead.

Jenny inhaled deeply as a surge of anger rushed through her. The adrenalin of hatred and the pain of despair forced out of her mouth as she screamed. She thrusted her naked body against the clear plastic capsule that held her in place. There was half an inch of clearance between her and the unbreakable bodycast, and she used that tiny space to expel her frustration.

She closed her eyes and screamed again but stopped her futile attempt to escape when she realised a new body had slid into Joshua's now empty capsule.

She was relieved she had missed the automated replacement. No matter how many times she had seen it, the sight of a dead body being sucked into the floor while a new person emerged from the ceiling always disturbed her.

It was quick, efficient and emotionless. A production line of misery.

"Hi, I'm Jenny," she offered to the terrified man beside her.

"What" he gasped.

"You're in the juicing factory... don't worry, it doesn't hurt," she smiled sadly.

"I know where I am!" he snapped back.

Jenny didn't reply. It was too soon for him. She would give it time.

After a few minutes of silence, the man looked over at Jenny's emaciated body. She looked like death. A malnourished, drained corpse. It surprised him she could speak.

"How long have you been here?" he asked.

"A while," she replied without looking at him. She couldn't bear to see the pity in his eyes.

Her defeat angered him. "Yeah, well, don't get used to me, Janine.

"Jenny," she corrected him.

He continued without acknowledgement. "There's no way in hell I'm staying here as long as you sweetheart. I'm going to get out of here."

She chuckled. The new ones always think they can beat the system.

"Oh?" she questioned.

The man nodded his head in response as he simultaneously scanned the warehouse sized room.

He looked beyond the never-ending rows of body filled capsules, his eyes searching for an exit. Not knowing that this room was one of a hundred others like it. Identical in layout. Identical in purpose. The entire building covering a square mile. His ignorance fuelled his confidence, and he looked determined as he thought through his situation. The man had not yet accepted his fate, but weeks from that day, he would. When his body stopped producing blood faster than they extracted it and he was too weak to fight, too tired to care, he would welcome death. But for now, he was resolute.

"I'm going to kill every last one of these bastards and I'm taking this blood sucking farm down with them!" he announced as Jenny lost consciousness for the final time, ending her reign as the longest living blood bag that year.

Chapter One

In the deserted heart of town, Arabelle stood amidst the aftermath of war, ebony hair pouring down her back like a midnight waterfall. Determination burned in her glamourous aquatic blue eyes, a stark contrast to the unwashed, makeup-free elegance of her face. She was a woman, curvaceous and sexy. She was a warrior, skilled in the Martial arts of combat. Poised for battle, she readied herself to confront a familiar adversary.

Before her stood a third generation BioBot, a marvel of modern technology and engineering. Its metallic frame glistened in the harsh sunlight, and its brown photoreceptor eyes scanned the surroundings, calculating every possible move.

The machine, in a former life as a security bot, had now become a formidable foe. Programmed for a single purpose: Get blood.

Arabelle clenched her fists, her short dirty fingernails digging into her palms. Knowing that every victory over a BioBot meant one step closer to safeguarding her people, her Kin, and their very existence of life, she steeled herself for the impending confrontation.

The wind picked up, swirling through the ruined town, creating a haunting melody that seemed to herald the impending battle.

The BioBot, flexed its mechanical joints, and a faint whirring sound filled the air as it prepared for combat. Arabelle took a deep breath, her chest rising and falling with each inhale and exhale. She stepped forward, her black leather boots crunching on the debris-covered ground.

"Come on," she screamed, her voice raspy with adrenalin.

Compliant to her demand, the BioBot lunged at her with incredible speed, its metal limbs protracted like deadly blades. Arabelle's reflexes were lightning-quick. She sidestepped the attack and delivered a powerful roundhouse kick to the robot's side. Her booted heel struck the metallic surface, creating a resounding clang that reverberated through her ears. Her foot instantly ached, and she shook her head at the stupidity of fighting a machine.

The impact sent the BioBot stumbling back, but it quickly regained its balance. It unleashed a barrage of ball bearing sized rubber bullets, designed to incapacitate not kill. A dead human didn't produce blood. Arabelle's lithe form danced and weaved through the searing beams, narrowly avoiding each impact.

With a swift motion, she drew her Katana, a blade she had forged from the steel of a beam she had found in an old warehouse some years ago. Its razor-sharp edge gleamed in the sunlight, ready for action. She charged toward The BioBot; her sword held high.

The BioBot responded with a powerful punch. Arabelle expertly rebounded the blow with her Katana, using her strength and skill to deflect the immense force. The impact sent sparks flying from the collision of metal on metal. She countered with a flurry of strikes, the blade of her Katana dancing through the air with grace and precision.

The BioBot's sensors detected her movements, and it adapted quickly. It extended its powerful arm, attempting to grapple

Arabelle. She skilfully tumbled away, narrowly escaping its clutches. As she landed gracefully, she swung her Katana, slicing off the extended arm with a shower of sparks and an explosion of black, coagulated human blood.

Arabelle smiled at her opponent. The presence of the old blood hinted at underlying dysfunction. At least forty-two days had passed since its last transfusion, leaving it in a critical state.

The BioBot staggered, but it was far from defeated. It unleashed another barrage of rubber bullets from its shoulder-mounted launcher. Arabelle's eyes widened, and she leaped into action, sprinting towards the robot with unparalleled speed fuelled by adrenaline. With her Katana in hand, Arabelle slashed through the air, her blade releasing a wave of energy that deflected the incoming missiles before they could reach her.

The BioBot was not discouraged. It stretched out its remaining arms as if to strangle Arabelle. She laughed. "Oh, you're that desperate, are you?" she mused.

She closed the distance between them and used the extended arm as a springboard to leap onto the BioBot's shoulders, Katana poised for a finishing blow.

However, The BioBot had one last trick up its mechanical sleeve. As it activated, a crackling sound filled the air, indicating the presence of its built-in electroshock defence system. Its surface crackled with electrical arcs, ready to deliver a powerful shock to anyone who dared touch it. Arabelle's eyes widened in pain as the electricity surged through her body, causing her muscles to convulse.

With a Herculean effort, she maintained her grip on her Katana and drove it into the BioBot's neck, severing its connection to the electroshock system and simultaneously opening a gash wide enough to bleed out its operating system.

The BioBot emitted a deafening, electronic scream as it sensed its demise. Closing her eyes, Arabelle focused on creating a mental barrier against the disruptive noise. The sound reminded her of a child's scream, she hated it. She wondered if the programmers intentionally designed them to sound that way, in an effort to make them more human, or if the BioBots modified the sound to evoke guilt in their attackers.

Guilt was such a human emotion.

The BioBot stumbled forward, its brown photoreceptor eyes flickering with uncertainty.

Arabelle leaped away from the disabled robot as it collapsed to the ground, defeated.

She panted heavily, the remnants of the electroshock still coursing through her veins. Her clothing charred and bloodied, and her body ached from the battle, but she had emerged victorious.

Serene silence enveloped the BioBot, its lifeless form contrasting with the echoes of the fierce confrontation that had unfolded, carried away by the wind.

Arabelle stood quietly amidst the wreckage of her town, a striking figure of determination and beauty. Her body, a perfect blend of allure and strength, bore scars of battles past, like delicate brushstrokes of clash etched on her ivory skin.

With her stunning looks and powerful intellect, she was both a goddess and a warrior. A symbol of bravery and power. A woman filled with fear and insecurity. Exhausted, she swayed on her feet, her eyes fixed on the fallen robot, understanding the fight was not yet over.

More challenges awaited her, more battles to protect her kin and her species. However, for the time being, she granted herself a brief respite, taking the opportunity to fully enjoy her hard-earned triumph and bask in the gratitude of another day that she did not die.

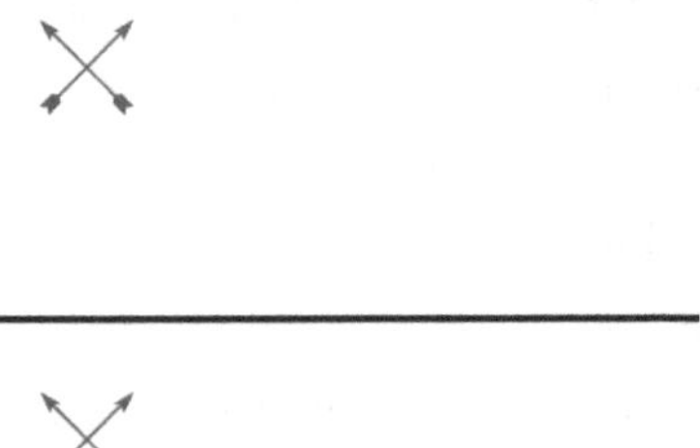

ARABELLE'S EYES SWEPT over the weathered facade of her modest home. The sight of her small, unassuming shack gave her a sense of relief. She made it home in one piece, grateful to be alive.

At first glance, the cabin seemed neglected and in disrepair, with broken windows and a crooked chimney. It looked perfectly designed for its purpose, as if it could be abandoned without any regret. The interior, much like the neglected exterior, exuded a sense of abandonment, but strangely, it was exactly what she needed.

Nestled on the outskirts of the kinship, it evaded notice, providing her with a cloak of isolation. It was a bold move, to live away from the others, but where most felt safety in numbers, Arabelle believed a solitary existence lowered the odds of becoming a target for blood-hungry assailants. As the top warrior of the Kin, she despised the idea of having to rescue others. 'Less people, less burden' was Arabelle's favourite motto, although she was known to break her own rules from time to time.

A stream of hot water embraced her in a soothing hug as she showered. It was such a simple pleasure, but left her vulnerable. She used to close her eyes when she showered, pleasured by the moisture on her skin. The cleansing of her body and the relaxation of her mind. Those were the days, the days before Hemovitalists had reached the New Zealand mainland.

Following the destructive Tri-species war that caused widespread chaos, the small island nation emerged largely unharmed. Despite their modest numbers, the resilient local human population remained untouched. In contrast to European nations, they refrained from crossing borders to intervene. The island's advantage lay in its fifteen thousand kilometres of coastline and the fact that the machines, which had a fear of water, made it an ideal protective barrier.

Hemovitalists were now the biggest threat. Word spread fast about a colony of humans on the isolated island. The blood bag as they become to be known, enough human to sustain Hemovitalists for decades. That was five years ago, and only a few hundred humans now survived. It seemed Hemovitalists had not lost all their human traits. Greed and rampant consumerism remained, driving their insatiable appetite for blood and power.

Arabelle emerged from the shower, droplets glistening on her skin like liquid crystals. She sat on a large floor cushion, feeling the breeze tickle her naked skin as she allowed it to dry her body. The rhythmic sound of her breath created a gentle cadence, inviting tranquillity. In this sacred moment, she navigated the currents of her mind, finding solace in the stillness.

Arabelle voiced the teachings of her Sifu, words she hesitated to accept, but found herself compelled to embrace, nonetheless.

"Strength bestowed, a shield I bear, to shield the weak with love and care."

Chapter Two

Dr. Stanley Cryton, an eccentric scientist renowned for his brilliant mind and distinctive unruly moustache, savoured the aroma of his plant-based bacon sandwich. He sniffed in the scent with a passion that suggested it was the first time he had ever encountered such a delightful smell. With an almost childlike enthusiasm, he pressed his nose against the freshly baked bread again, inhaling as though the very essence of life emanated from this culinary creation. It was his usual Sunday treat, a treat he gave himself as consolation for working on the weekend. Truth be told, he worked seven days a week, but this little ritual marked the occasion enough to make him feel like his life was still worthwhile.

Briskly, he swung open the door to his cluttered laboratory, a space that had become a second home. A place of solitude and scientific endeavours over the course of eight years. The room, though devoid of human presence, was alive with the humming machines, Dr Cryton's only companions in his pursuit of success.

A success that he could or not, or rather, would not explain to anyone. The soothing blue glow emitted by the flickering computer screens welcomed him. A silent partner to the countless experiments and the tireless pursuit of a breakthrough.

Addressing the empty laboratory as if it were a long-time companion, Dr. Cryton grinned and exclaimed, "Good morning, Barry! Are you bloody good?"

For eight years, the Blood Analytics Replication Intelligence Expert, affectionately known as B.A.R.I.E, dutifully responded with a robotic monotony, delivering the same disheartening message, 'Negative, Stan Cryton, we have unviable results.' Overnight analysis was common. When he wore a younger man's clothes, Dr. Stanley Cryton would sit by B.A.R.I.E, willing the result, willing a viable outcome. Now, he would go home, sleep a little, eat a lot and worry about B.A.R.I.E. He would lay awake hoping it to find the correct result.

Hope was not a scientific measure, but some days it was all he had to keep him going.

For eight years, every morning, "Negative, Stan Cryton, we have unviable results." It had become a routine, a ritual of disappointment.

Today, as the scent of his plant-based bacon sandwich filled the room, the routine was shattered. B.A.R.I.E, the mechanical companion that had shared countless unfruitful experiments with Dr. Cryton, broke its usual script and uttered words that stop time and resonated with profound significance.

"Yes, Stan Cryton, we have viable results."

Dr. Stanley Cryton's fingers suddenly stopped working. The plate, carrying his plant-based bacon sandwich, slipped from his grasp, and shattered on the floor. He stood there, momentarily stunned, in complete silence.

He had never even considered the possibility of achieving a viable result, as the dream had always remained ever-present. But what would happen on the day that a viable result is actually found? He stood there, silent, and unsure, pondering his next move.

His mind raced, seeking the right response for the moment—perhaps a humorous anecdote, a 'one small step for man' speech, or just any words at all. However, only one thing occupied his thoughts.

He looked over at a photograph of his wife and daughter, noting the stark contrast in their expressions from the last time he saw them. In that frozen moment, their faces reflected happiness, untouched by the agony and sorrow inflicted by disease. Their smiles radiated joy and youthfulness, blissfully unaware of the motivation their deaths would later offer.

A twinkle of joy lit up his eyes, a familiar reaction whenever he caught a glimpse of his wife.

"I've done it, my love. I've done it," he whispered as a smile emerged from behind his bushy moustache.

Dr. Stan Cryton, on the day of his scientific breakthrough in finding a single cure for every blood-borne disease that plagued humanity, was in a moment of reflection. He knelt down, a sense of accomplishment mingled with a hint of regret, as he began the delicate task of picking up the scattered fragments of his favourite plate and the remnants of his plant-based bacon sandwich.

The man whose intellect had unlocked the secrets of hematology, now found himself dealing with the ordinary act of cleaning up the aftermath of a small mishap.

'

The mirror backstage of the Elysian Apex Auditorium reflected a figure clad in a meticulously chosen suit, every crease and fold, a silent affirmation of the gravity of the day. The reflection captured a man on the verge of transforming the world, with a blend of nerves and determination obvious in his eyes.

Ten years had passed since his groundbreaking discovery, and today marked the peak of that scientific journey. The sceptical atmosphere in the auditorium did little to ease Dr. Stanley Cryton's nerves as he cleared his throat for the third time in less than a minute. Today was to be thrilling, yet the acid pit in his stomach stifled any excitement he should have felt.

A shiny silver humanoid ascended the stairs to the stage with deliberate steps, catching the attention of the audience.

It greeted them with enthusiasm, waving and giving a cheeky wink at Dr. Cryton, who anxiously awaited backstage.

"Great to see you all," it announced, drawing the audience's immediate attention.

The aspiration to bring forth a cyborg had been impeded by the introduction of morality laws that imposed restrictions on the application of human tissue. However, this machine, powered by blood, emerged as the next best thing.

"Great question," the humanoid responded with an enthusiastic thumbs up.

"My name is Barry. I am a BioBot, and thanks to you, I can detect and respond to biological stimuli in real time."

A resounding applause filled the auditorium.

Dr. Cryton wiped the sweat from his forehead, feeling as if he had sent an innocent child into battle. So far, the BioBot was holding its own, charming the audience as it was programmed to do.

"I could wear clothes if you want me to, but I have zero fashion sense."

Laughter filled the room, and Dr. Cryton's shoulders slumped in relief. Sending the BioBot out on its own had been a gamble, and until this moment, he was unsure whether it would work for or against his cause. While androids were widely accepted, the idea of creating a blood-based fuel source was considered a controversial leap.

Dr. Cryton tirelessly advocated for this groundbreaking concept in interviews, news articles, and conversations, highlighting the potential for donor organ growth and increased human longevity. When faced with the unknown, humanity did what it always did - it became scared and sceptical.

Barry, the BioBot, effortlessly captivated the audience with his charm and articulate speech. The idea of an artificial intelligence surpassing, outwitting, and outfighting humans appeared remote to them. The charm and eloquence of Barry masked the imminent danger posed by an artificial intelligence with such capabilities. The once-present fear of this threat had now faded into a distant afterthought for the spectators.

"Let's bring him out shall we," Barry announced.

Dr. Stanley Cryton vigorously shook his entire body, as though attempting to physically cast off the nerves that gripped him. "Let's do this," he encouraged himself, taking a determined step into the spotlight.

Barry enveloped him in a warm hug, playfully slapping his back like an old friend.

The transition from the auditorium to real-world application would take months, not years. Humans would not just rely on the

BioBots; they would come to love them. Along the way, learning a valuable lesson–always read the small print.

Disclaimer: Cryton Industries explicitly declares and delineates that it shall bear no legal responsibility nor assume liability for any actions, deeds, or consequences arising from the deployment and utilisation of a BioBot subsequent to its reassignment to a new user, thereby absolving the company from any legal ramifications associated therewith.

Barry clapped his shiny metal hand together gleefully. "Look, Daddy is here,"

The entire audience stood up and applauded in a standing ovation.

Chapter Three

HANGING LOW IN THE night sky, the moon appeared like a celestial lantern, casting a weak glow that bathed the abandoned town in an ethereal and pale shade.

Arabelle walked cautiously along a narrow laneway, hoping to find something, anything, she could use to repair and fortify her Kin's village. The new world suited her just fine. No bustling crowds, no pushy individuals—just the world at her feet, awaiting her every command. It was a land of solitude, where she could relish the quiet and enjoy the freedom to seize whatever lay before her.

Before she could see the source, she heard the rhythmic breathing and instinctively paused, tilting her head to pinpoint its location.

Christchurch city, or what remained, was the best scavenging ground, only four hours' walk from her Kinship. It was closest but also the most dangerous. BioBots frequented the area on blood hunts and Hemovitalists lived in the high-rise building basements car parks. Preferring the dark, secure, and defendable position. Arabelle hated them with a passion, but had to admire their tactical adaptability.

In this desolate scene, the once-grand high-rises stood as mere shells of their former glory, while the streets below were strewn with the remnants of a world that had been torn apart.

Arabelle tuned into the breathing sound.

It was too loud to be human and too artificial to be a Hemovitalist. It was definitely a BioBot, using its stereo breathing sound as intimidation.

Arabelle raised her Katana slowly. She had not seen the mechanical menace but by the sounds of it; it had seen her. Why is it waiting to attack? She thought to herself as she turned to meet her adversary. In the dimly lit battleground at the end of the laneway, the soft moonlight exposed the BioBot, poised ready to fight... with its back to Arabelle.

Confused, her eyes searched the shadows for its potential enemy, as it was not her who posed the threat.

A man came into view, a commanding presence that effortlessly seized attention. His towering frame eclipsed the six-foot mark, each contour of his physique a testament to disciplined strength. Broad shoulders demanding respect, leading down to a powerful, firm chest that hinted at untapped potential. His long, muscular legs suggested a potential for dynamic movement, complementing his overall physique.

Arabelle paused to admire him. Physicality, he was not a display of brute force; it was an artful composition of muscle tone, proportion, and overall fitness. There was no excess bulk nor undue leanness, but a captivating equilibrium that made him a spectacle of aesthetic allure.

With no human settlements nearby, he must have ventured from a more distant location. In the subtle play of shadows, he stood like a living sculpture. Arabelle could not look away.

"Oh, hello handsome," she whispered in an uncharacteristically flirtatious voice. "I suppose I better save your cute little arse,"

A palpable tension charged the air, gripping every breath as the adversaries' locked eyes.

Handsome, with his flawless arrangement of features. Shoulder-length sandy blonde hair framing a face that spoke more of passion than combat. And the Biobot, a second generation combat ready personal protection model. Nothing fancy, built for home security.

Arabelle watched intently, preparing herself for the moment when she would need to step in to rescue another soul teetering on the brink of mortal peril. Her eyes focusing on the emerald-green eyes gaze of handsome as he stared down his opponent with a look that, oddly, seemed to invite connection rather than confrontation.

Suddenly, he made the first move, darting with unnatural speed and superhuman agility. He launched himself at the BioBot, aiming for a lethal strike at the robot's metallic throat.

The BioBot, was not caught off guard. Its advanced sensors had detected Handsome's movement and reacted with machine-like precision.

The robot sidestepped the attack, avoiding the deadly strike by a hair's breadth and in one swift motion, delivered a powerful punch to the Hemovitalists jaw, the sheer force of it causing Handsome to stagger backwards.

Arabelle found herself facing two adversaries in this battle—the BioBot and, unmistakably now, a Hemovitalist. She took a deep breath, preparing to interject, but then corrected her line of thought. Wait to see who wins and then you have only one to kill.

She rolled her eyes at her own stupidity and stepped back into the shadows to wait.

Handsome stood again, waiting to attack. His posture, a testament to innate confidence, exuded relaxation despite the impending encounter with the biologically engineered, blood-starved machine. Arabelle felt both drawn and conflicted — a mortal enemy stirring feelings of desire. It didn't feel right.

Handsome charged headlong at the BioBot, his resolve firm to topple the massive mechanical beast. Their collision sent shockwaves through the air as he collided with it forcefully. The BioBot retaliated by clamping down on Handsome's torso, attempting to crush him within its metallic grip. Handsome, not to be outdone, utilised his free arm to tear and rip at the BioBot's exterior, aiming to disable its mechanical might.

Handsome expertly wriggled out of the machine's grasp, capitalising on his lower position to seize its ankles and apply a forceful tug in an attempt to destabilise it. Unfortunately, his efforts were in vain. As he received a resounding blow to the top of his head, he managed to grasp the inner thigh of the robot and tear off a piece of artificial flesh.

They exchanged blows, punching and shoving each other like a schoolyard brawl, before they regained their composure and transitioned into a more professional fighting stance.

Both adversaries were showing signs of wear and fatigue, but they were equally determined to emerge victorious. Their strength was evenly matched, and they pushed against each other, each trying to gain the upper hand. Handsome's superhuman strength was pitted against the BioBot's mechanical power. The battle of wills continued, each side locked in a stalemate, unable to gain the upper hand.

The BioBot lunged forward, attempting to grapple with handsome, but he was quicker still, using his agility to slip away and deliver a punishing roundhouse kick to its metal chest. The BioBot stumbled back, crashing on its knees but refusing to yield. As handsome approached the BioBot, it used its powerful arms to lift its body and double kick Handsome's legs out from under him. Handsome let out a yelp of pain.

"You mechanical fuckwit!" he yelled at the BioBot, like it would make a difference for the machine to hear his insult.

Summoning his last reserves of strength, the Hemovitalist regained his feet. With grim determination, he reached for the hilt of a hidden dagger strapped to his side. In a desperate act, he launched himself at the BioBot, the dagger flashing in the dim light. It hardly had time to react, and the blade found its mark, slicing into its soft stomach region. The BioBot cried out in fake pre-programed pain, stumbling backward as it clutched its wound.

Handsome shook his head, unimpressed by the emotional tactic.

The battle had taken an unexpected turn, and the ground was now level.

Both warriors stood battered and wounded, their resolve unwavering.

As Arabelle stood there, her body became tense with anticipation, knowing deep down that this fight was one she had invested her emotions in, much like the intense anticipation one feels while spectating a grudge match.

The mechanical fighter made a swift advance, trying to engage with the handsome figure, but he proved to be faster, deftly evading its reach. With a last burst of agility, he executed a devastating punch to the metallic face of the BioBot. It took the full impact with no emotion and returned the punch likewise. A robotic blow to Handsome's chiselled jaw and his eyes flashed with fury.

Momentarily stunned, he regained his composure and summoned his immense strength and resilience once more. This battle was far from over. His long experience in combat had taught him the art of adaptation, and he knew he needed to be more strategic if he were to defeat this mechanical adversary. Blow for blow, they were at a stalemate.

The handsome Hemovitalist abruptly retreated, as if running scared. The BioBot stood still. To chase could lead to a trap. It slowly turned, scanning its surroundings. Arabelle crouched down low when it circled around in her direction. She too scanned the surroundings for handsome. Surely, he had not run away in fear.

The BioBot stopped scanning. Now, it had Arabelle directly in its line of sight.

Suddenly, with a silent grace, Handsome emerged from the shadows, his eyes gleaming with malevolence. He launched a surprise attack, lunging at BioBot from behind. With his strong fingers extended, he aimed for the back of the robot's neck, hoping to strike a lethal blow. Tearing at the wires threaded behind its skull, the Hemovitalist continued his frenzied attack. The BioBot reached over his shoulder, grabbed the Hemovitalist hard and slammed him down into the concrete, shattering the footpath. Handsome was winded, struggling to compose himself. The BioBot sensed victory and raised its leg, ready to crush Handsome's face.

Handsome used the last of his energy to punch away the leg and execute a perfect technical stand-up. Then, with a single swift motion, he brought done the knife into the BioBot soft brown eye. He stabbed violently over and over as the BioBot punched his ribs; each blow lessened with strength the deeper handsome drove his blade into the operating system. The Biobot's screams were deafening, Arabelle covered her ears to stop the screeching pain in them. The Hemovitalist, unaffected by the sound, continued to thrash at the BioBot's eye socket, long after his opponent had ceased punching. Handsome stood up and took a deep, cleansing breath.

The battle was over.

Arabelle's heart sank as she realized the Hemovitalist had emerged victorious. Although taking down a BioBot was no easy feat, living with its demise was a lot easier to do.

The Hemovitalist was tired; she had a better chance of victory. The time was now. She rolled her shoulders, tighten the grip on her weapon and confidently step forward, exposing her position.

Handsome turned and faced her. He had never seen such a beautiful combatant. She looked fierce, yet vulnerable.

He sensed she could kill him, but he already felt wounded by her eyes. What a magnificent creature.

"I'm Quillian." he said loudly, his face neutral and calm.

"I don't give a fuck," Arabelle shouted back.

He smiled; she was awesome. "Did you like the show?" he asked excitedly.

Arabelle did not respond.

"You know, we don't have to fight," he suggested.

Arabelle snorted. "Yeah, great idea, why don't I just lay down and you can suck me dry," she defiantly replied.

Quillian grinned mischievously. "Or, consider this, I could be the one who lies down and you could ..." he stopped short of offending a lady.

Arabelle's brow furrowed. Is this Hemo flirting with me?... Before she had time to understand what was happening, he gave her a winked and was gone.

A moment passed. Arabelle giggled. She wasn't sure why.

Perhaps it was the overwhelming sense of relief that she didn't have to engage in a life-or-death battle, or perhaps it was the experience of encountering the one and only man who made her truly feel like a genuine woman.

Chapter Four

ARABELLE WAS ASTONISHED to find herself a mere two hundred meters from the human village, yet the full extent of the structures remained hidden from her sight. It was always a surprised to see how well the chosen spot was working to their advantage.

From that distance, the homes of over fifty residents appeared hidden within the rainforest, giving the impression of a barely inhabited clearing. A few tiny cottages were concealed behind a giant mountain ash eucalypt, while a rocky outcrop veiled four family homes. The tree-covered hillside encircling the outer perimeter had small door-like structures concealed in the undergrowth. Arabelle admired the ingenuity of the work. Concealing the cavernous dwellings behind seemingly unassuming, grass-covered entryways was clever. The doors would remain undetected at night and easily overlooked during the day.

This charming and quaint settlement, cocooned by the emerald canopy of towering trees and perpetually enshrouded by mist, offered an ideal shelter for a modest number of humans seeking housing and seclusion. It indicated human resilience, harmony with the environment, and the acceptance of a simpler way of life.

The locals affectionately refer to it as 'Uronga,' while the Hemovitalists had dubbed it 'The Blood Bank.'

The largest pocket of humans on the South Island.

At first glance, it appears to be an enchanting paradise secluded from the hustle and bustle of the outside world. However, accessing the true centre of the village was possible only via a complex network of serpentine trails that wound their way through the lush rainforest. These pathways not only provide a means of access, but also serve as a defensive tactic, channelling potential threats into a single, manageable route.

The moment you set foot in Uronga, cradled by nature, the air itself seemed to radiate with a sense of tranquillity. Weathered rocks, shaped by the hands of mother nature, stood as silent sentinels, guarding the essence of home. Hardwood, sourced from the nearby forests, weaved into structures, telling stories of seasons past and those yet to come. The buildings, with their traditional architecture, showcase a design refined by countless sunsets and rain showers.

The narrow windows, shy yet purposeful, allow glimpses of life inside the structures. They open the door to natural ventilation, inviting the ever-present whispers of the wind and the soothing pitter-patter of rain. The architectural marvels of Uronga embody the community's ancestral knowledge, transforming it into a captivating living art. The village not only told the story of resilience, but it also conveyed the importance of self-sufficiency. With every weathered stone to every repurposed beam. It was a salvage of a community that used to be.

A clearing amidst the village of Uronga served as a communal gathering area, known as the heart of the village. A circle of towering trees, their roots serving as natural seats, with the overhead canopy cleverly offering natural camouflage surrounded the meeting area.

Returning home without supplies was disappointing, and having to kill a BioBot on an empty stomach had only added to Arabelle's bad mood. She stomped into her best friend's home and threw her knapsack onto the unmade bed in the corner of the small room. Making her way over to the fireplace, which was nothing more than a half drum propped up on mud bricks, Arabelle was always amazed at how effectively it warmed up the entire living area, even during the most frigid nights. The embers were almost extinguished, and she groaned at yet another frustration, having to lecture Madlyn about keeping the firewood stocked.

The kitchen was a mess. The droppings on the table revealed that an unwelcome visitor had consumed the remaining food. She didn't bother to check inside the cupboard.

"What a day," she sighed as she flicked the little black pellets onto the mosaic tiled floor.

"Please, do come in," Madlyn replied sarcastically.

Madlyn was a plump, jovial woman, radiating happiness from within. Her impossibly long blonde hair framed a mature and timeless face. Despite being only in her early twenties, she possessed a beauty that transcended age, showcased by her mesmerizing brown eyes, luscious lips, and prominent cheekbones. Madlyn's small yet strong physique gave the impression she was capable of protecting both herself and the people she held dear.

Unlike Arabelle, who enjoyed housework, Madlyn had a strong aversion to it and instead thrived in social situations, showcasing her outgoing nature. Being in the company of others brought out the best in her and she effortlessly formed and nurtured strong relationships thanks to her exceptional listening skills. Arabelle both loved and hated that about her. Madlyn had always been protective and had a kind-hearted nature, always putting the needs of others before her own. She not only excelled at being a superb cook but was also quick-witted, adding a touch of humour to every gathering. Her overall personality was a delightful blend of positivity, kindness, and a zest for life that had an uplifting effect on those fortunate enough to be around her.

"Why do you live like such a pig" Arabelle asked the same rhetorical question every time she visited.

"Why are you such a control freak?" Madlyn responded.

Arabelle couldn't recall a time when Madlyn wasn't a fixture in her life. Neither of them could remember when they first met. They had always just been. Confidantes from the start, they shared dreams, fears, and aspirations. Triumphs were shared with joy, losses mourned as one, and they stood shoulder to shoulder through a life of war and heartbreak. Although opposite in nature they complemented each other rather than clashed. Arabelle's strength and fortitude served as a steadfast shield, preserving Madlyn's compassion and generosity. On the other hand, Madlyn's idealistic optimism provided a gentle counterbalance to Arabelle's determination and pragmatism.

They had become pillars in each other's lives from time immemorial, understanding a shared history that only they could appreciate. As the years turned into decades, Arabelle and Madlyn found themselves embraced by a friendship that exuded a comforting warmth, fortified by an unbreakable trust.

"Control freak!?" Arabelle playfully retorted "If it wasn't for me..."

"I could be as reckless as a penguin trying to break-dance on an iceberg," Madlyn finished.

Arabelle's eyebrows raised as she tried to comprehend such a random analogy. "What in the hell are you talking about" She laughed.

Madlyn shrugged her shoulders. "I dunno. I'm just a penguin," she replied with a cheeky grin.

Madlyn was unintentionally sexy and while men might have been drawn to her like moths to a flame, her heart belonged to only one. Verity was not only her lover but also her life partner. In the Kin, they were a loving couple, compatible with everyone, with one notable exception—Verity held a deep-seated aversion towards Annabelle, and was the only person in the Kin that hated her protection.

"Well how about my little fat penguin gives me a hand at cleaning up this pigsty?" Arabelle teased.

Madlyn scrunched up her face and defiantly poked out her tongue.

Chapter Five

ARABELLE HESITATED at the edge of her neatly made bed, her fingers gingerly tracing the rough fabric of her combat-ready clothes. She never dared to undress for sleep; the very notion felt like a luxury from a distant past. The worn, olive-green fabric clung to her shapely frame, a constant companion borne out of instinct, a shield against the ever-looming threat of an attack, whether it be in the blinding daylight or the dead of night.

A pain filled sigh escaped her lips as she cast a wistful glance towards the once inviting bed. The sheets, now untouched and neatly tucked, held the memory of a time when she could indulge in the simple pleasures of spreading her legs freely without the constricting grip of underwear, the tight embrace of pants, or the persistent weight of her boots. Those sensations were ghosts of a life surrendered to the relentless vigilance demanded by her now perilous existence.

The room, lit by a flickering lantern, had the telltale signs of a makeshift survivor. A dresser, scarred by time and repurposed from a world that was no more, stood in the corner. Its cracked mirror reflected the weariness etched on Annabelle's beautiful face, a suggestion of the toll of ceaseless nights spent in combat-ready attire. With a sense of resignation, Arabelle settled onto the bed, her body tense despite the apparent comfort.

She lay in stillness, eyes fixed on the ceiling above, the anticipation of sleep hanging over her. Tempting but never fully realised. The hushed sounds of the night outside whispered of potential dangers lurking beyond the fragile walls of her refuge. Her gaze lingered on the ceiling, as if searching for answers in its worn surface. A heavy truth pressed upon her—despite the resilience of her kin and the fiery determination that fuelled her own spirit, humanity teetered on the brink of extinction. No amount of vigilance, no heroic stand, seemed capable of halting the unstoppable slide toward total elimination.

Sleep, when it arrived, offered little solace. The respite it brought was brief, like catching a fleeting breath amid an unyielding storm. Yet, on most nights, she managed to secure around five precious hours of slumber. Tonight mirrored the familiar pattern, the cycle of restless thoughts and fleeting rest persisting.

Helplessness settled over her like a heavy fog, obscuring her thoughts. The chilly night a partner in her quiet battle against a destiny that appeared to resist any attempts to alter it.

IN QUILLIAN'S LUXURIOUS bedroom, filled with gentle lighting, the air was scented with a delicate blend of lavender and vanilla. The room was a testament to timeless beauty, with rich tapestries, stolen from the finest of homes, adorned the walls, and polished mahogany furniture adding an air of elegance. The canopy bed, dressed in layers of silk and Egyptian cotton, beckoned with promises of indulgent comfort.

Hemovitalist understood that strength is the catalyst for acquiring power, and with that power, one gains the ability to seize the most exquisite odds and ends that remain in the world.

Quillian, dressed in luxurious silk pyjamas that whispered with each stride. Every step sent a jolt of pain through his battered body. He found comfort knowing that by morning, the Hemo virus would have worked its restorative magic. The delicate chandelier overhead cast a warm radiance on the scene, highlighting the sumptuous surroundings. As he approached the bed, the plush velvet and embroidered pillows invited touch, promising a haven of opulence and tranquillity.

With intentional yet smooth actions, Quillian gently lifted the duvet, exposing the indulgent sheets beneath. The mattress, soft and inviting, gave way beneath his weight, cradling him in comfort. The drapes of the canopy were drawn closed, cocooning the sleeper in an intimate enclave of serenity, shutting out the outside world.

Reclining against the plump pillows, Quillian's handsome features softened into a serene expression. The pain, though not forgotten, gradually faded into the soft bed. Muted tones and lavish textures surrounded him, creating an atmosphere of quiet satisfaction. The room itself seemed to cradle Quillian, as if acknowledging the need for respite and to offer a reward for being almighty. The faint rustle of fine fabrics, barely audible, became the only sound breaking the silence as Quillian succumbed to the embrace of a well-deserved slumber. Now, the space was a sanctuary of quietude. The only movement was the gentle rise and fall of Quillian's chest, as he was rewarded with another night of deep and undisturbed sleep.

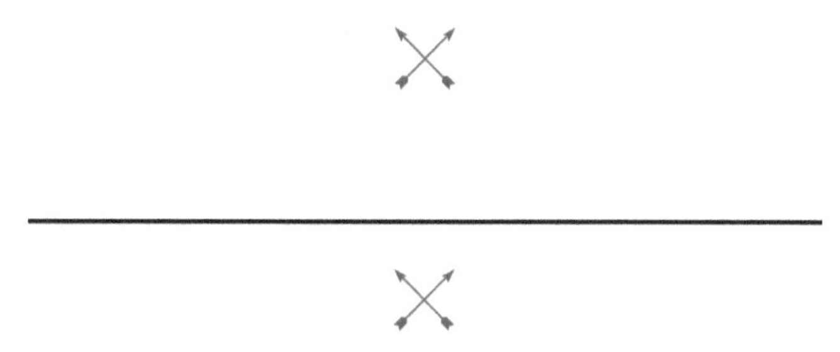

MADLYN UNABASHEDLY disrobed in the presence of Verity, displaying a confidence and pride in her body that was undeniably her sexiest trait. Verity, who had already intimately explored every contour of Madlyn's form, appeared somewhat indifferent to the unveiling. Her eyes shifted from the exposed figure before her just in time to see Madlyn sliding under the sheets of their shared bed.

The dim light in their eclectic bedroom flickered, casting uneven shadows on the worn-out plasterboard that clung desperately to the uneven framework. Faded photographs nailed to the cracked walls and a solitary, tattered teddy bear sat silently on a wooden chair, its varnish now faded to a warm, honeyed patina. A thick air, saturated with a blend of mustiness and the distant fragrance of scavenged candles, was present, contributing to an atmosphere that seemed to mirror the uncertainty beyond the walls.

Remaining engrossed in her worn-out book, its tattered pages captivating her attention, Verity nonchalantly voiced a weighty question, "Is this us forever?"

In response, Madlyn paused, considering the inquiry. "What do you mean?" she asked; her curiosity roused.

Without lifting her eyes from the text, Verity calmly articulated her concerns, "Living day to day, hoping not to be captured, hoping not be killed, hoping not to be sucked dry, scavenging for supplies... you know, this basic existence forced on us from the past and now without a future..."

The creaky floor beneath the bed added an eerie echo to their conversation as Madlyn reached out her hand towards Verity. Their fingers intertwined with a firm grip, finding comfort in the tactile connection amid the uncertainty. However, instead of offering words of comfort or hope for a brighter future, Madlyn released a sigh tinged with hopelessness.

With raw honesty, she replied, "Yes, this is us forever."

Chapter Six

THE MORNING SUN STREAMED through the sheer holey curtains, casting a warm glow on the quaint kitchen at Madlyn's place. The air was filled with the comforting scent of freshly ground coffee beans, embracing the room. The table was cluttered with mismatched vintage dishes and colourful cloth napkins, creating a welcoming and homely atmosphere.

Madlyn was a vivacious host with a twinkle in her eye, she moved elegantly between the wood fire stove and the countertop, orchestrating a symphony of breakfast delights. The sizzle of freshly laid eggs hitting the pan and the rhythmic clinking of utensils against bowls harmonised with her cheerful morning chatter.

As Madlyn plated the breakfast dishes, each one became a work of art. An omelette, carefully seasoned with diced capsicum, spinach, and cherry tomatoes, rested on a chipped ceramic plate. The homemade jams, with their secret ingredient of love, neatly arranged in small glass jars, added a personal touch to the scene.

Arabelle sat attentively at the table, her stomach growling in anticipation of the nourishing feast that awaited her. The only proper meal she would eat each day was Madlyn's famous homecooked breakfast. It was a ritual she never missed.

Arabelle swung herself around to face the door and rested her hand on the grip of the large sword that hung from her waist belt. She was never without it, and although people joked that she looked like she was part of an old-fashioned Calvary; she was so skilled with the blade she could see no sense in replacing it.

She listened intently, trying to identify the steps. Single, two-legged creature about seven metres south from the cabin entrance. Walking at pace, showing no fear. Not sneaking up. Confident stride.

"You expecting company?" she asked urgently.

Madlyn rolled her eyes. "Yes, I am Captain Paranoid, Verity is coming back from the field,"

Arabelle did not relax.

Madlyn laughed. "Stand down before you kill my girlfriend."

Arabelle kicked opened the door.

"What the hell Belle!" Madlyn protested.

Her anger quickly distracted by the fear of an unknown intruder.

The silver humanoid figure stopped walking and waited for Arabelle to react. Both BioBot and Human stood still, assessing the situation. Arabelle looked over its stainless-steel body with interest. She normally didn't get the time to look closely at them.

It was an older model, still strong, but very much outdated. It had a female form, with the shape and contours of a sex-bot, but none of the anatomy. Despite being unarmed, it did not seem cautious as it stood helpless, like a lamb sent to the slaughter. BioBots rarely travelled alone and Arabelle didn't care to find out why this one seemed different.

Arabelle pulled the sword slowly from its sheath and rushed towards the BioBot. With one powerful move, she separated its head from its body. The expression on its synthetic skinned face didn't change as the skull rolled across the ground in front of her. The robotic body stood as motionless, just as it had been since Arabelle first appeared.

Arabelle looked down at the perfectly proportioned face. It was artificially beautiful and made no sense why it would sacrifice itself. It was not logical.

"Stupid fucking machine," Arabelle grunted as she kicked the body to the ground. Just as the torso landed, a group of four BioBots appeared from the tree line. While constantly watching and assessing the situation, the decoy served as a tool to lure out the enemy.

Arabelle shook her head at the cruelty. "Oh, wow we are evolving, aren't we?" she teased.

The BioBots spread themselves equally apart, assuming the attack formation. Arabelle had seen it countless times before. 'So predictable,' she thought as she steadied herself, ready for battle. She knew the far left one would rush past her and check the cabin for more humans. The far-right one would stay back and only approach when she was preoccupied with the two middle ones who always attacked first. As expected, and without emotion, the two middle BioBots lunged towards her. The fight was on.

Arabelle leaped catlike at her opponents, waving her sword in infinity pattern kata several times before landing at their feet. The first Bot to make contact was easily disabled. Arabelle's sharp blade sliced off its arms as it tried to grab her throat. Disarmed but not dead, it stumbled around, leaning against her as she plunged her sword into the body of her second combatant. Cutting and tearing the primary operation system into a nonfunctional mess.

She struggled to pull her sword from its torso as the full weight of its mechanical form slumped onto her arm.

A sharp pain in her back and the air burst from her lungs, leaving Arabelle unable to breathe. She turned towards the source of the blunt force impact to see the first BioBot had now steadied itself and was kicking her from behind.

She wrenched the sword out of its dead companion and skilfully dropped to the ground, spreading one leg to her side to create balance as she reached back with both arms and swung the sword through the legs of her armless adversary. It thudded to the ground and Arabelle jumped onto its back, ripping back its head and stabbed her fingers into the soft gauze under its chin, pulling out the main supply unit from its casing.

Dizzy from lack of oxygen, Arabelle slumped onto the ground and focused on drawing breath. Her lungs opened, and she gulped in a lifesaving breath as she listened to the pounding sound of a running BioBot.

"Fair dinkum." she whispered as she rose to her feet.

She dropped her sword and ran towards the machinery in motion. She knew the impact would hurt, but in the thick of the fight she thought nothing of battle scars. The two forces met with a sickening thud. The weight of the robotic mass pushing Arabelle's feet deep into the soil as she stood firm.

She drove her elbow deep into the BioBot's chest plate. She knew from experience that despite looking to the contrary, the plates were thin aluminium and easily penetrated. The eyes of her rival closed, and it fell to the ground. Arabelle tucked her grazed and bloodied arm close to her chest for protection and scanned the area for any other attacks. All Clear.

Arabelle sat down on the ground, surrounded by the remains of the artificial lives she had taken. She sucked the cool morning air into her lungs and tried to compose herself as the adrenaline rushed through her body. She felt like she wanted to cry and laugh and scream, all at the same time. Tears from the fear, triumphant laughter at winning and outcry at the resentment of a never-ending battle for survival.

The emotions of victory, as always, were bittersweet.

"You know such a small group, like four BioBots wouldn't normally attack a village our size. You are just asking for trouble living out there by yourself." Madlyn calmly stated as she walked up to Arabelle unfazed by the surrounding carnage.

Arabelle smiled. Despite not being the kind of person to have friends, she found Madlyn was her type of people. Calm and grounded, she was a voice of reason in an unsound world. Combining a quirky beauty with humility and kindness. She was the best of humanity.

"Oh look, she arrives right after I could have used her help," Arabelle smirked, hiding the pain she was in for the sake of her friend.

Madlyn grinned. "My help! Yeah right, like you needed help to slice up these old tin cans,"

Arabelle frowned. "Four?" she questioned.

Madlyn looked confused. "Four what?"

"You said four BioBots wouldn't attack. There were five." She answered as she looked over at Madlyn's cottage. "Excuse me for a second,"

Arabelle picked up her sword and marched over to the cabin and kicked the door open, swinging her weapon and screaming as she stormed into the room like a one-woman army.

Madlyn flinched and grimaced as she heard the battle from inside continue for over a minute. The clashing of utensils, thundering footsteps, and the occasional roar of combatants burst from the cabin, intensifying the grim reality of warfare. An abrupt scream and explosive bang and then silence.

As she cautiously retreated, her eyes fixed on the dark doorway, she found herself in a state of suspense, anxiously awaiting the arrival of the victor, only to be relieved by the unexpected sound of a voice she knew well, resonating from the depths of the darkness.

"I fucking hate those BioBastards!" Arabelle exclaimed as she limped into view.

Madlyn laughed. "Well, they hate you too, you know."

Arabelle walked towards her, each step carefully taken to mask the pain she was concealing.

"You okay" Madlyn asked.

"I'll be fine, but I don't like what I see here. Broad daylight, such a small group, it's too brazen, too risky for their logic. They are becoming desperate Mad; you better call a Kin meeting."

Chapter Seven

WITH THE HELP OF HER flawlessly sculpted, round derriere, Shyla delicately nudged the door open and seductively backed into the room.

Her striking beauty was a direct contrast to her nefarious intentions. Her tall and statuesque figure exuded confidence and power. Except for some strategically placed light freckles on her nose and upper cheeks, her complexion was flawless. The most captivating aspect of her appearance was her eyes.

Deep and mesmerizing, their unique shade of Emerald Green, hinting at a touch of malevolence. They were framed by long, inky-black lashes, giving her stare an irresistible intensity. Her hair, a vibrant shade of crimson red, flowed down her back in long, silky waves. She often styled it in a way that accentuated her face's elegant features, with a few tendrils falling artfully around her sharp cheekbones.

Shyla was never underdressed and today was no exception. Her attire was both glamorous and provocative. A sleek black designer cocktail dress that highlighted her figure, while her stiletto boots highlighted her well-proportioned legs.

The office was unusually dark for the time of day, but there was enough light that she could see the handsome man sitting at the desk.

Even though he was sitting, she could see how tall he was. There was no hiding his 6-foot 4-inch frame. She stopped at the door, just for a moment to admire him. His sandy hair and pale green eyes. His square jaw and strong cheekbones.

His smooth skin and well portioned nose. Her eyes stopped at his mouth and the exaggerated cupid's bow. It spoilt the fullness of his lips, but was cute and quirky at the same time. It was the only flaw in an otherwise perfect masculine face. She never grew tired of looking at him. Three years working by his side and his handsomeness still took her by surprise. She drew in a deep breath to cleanse the dirty thoughts from her mind.

"Oh Quillan," she announced as she entered the room. "Your dinner is ready."

He didn't look up, engrossed in the book he was reading.

She pushed the wheelchair into the centre of the room, leaving it there while she walked behind his chair.

Quillan had no illusion when it came to his personal assistant. He knew she was in love with him and despite doing nothing to encourage or reciprocate her affections, she still insisted on treating him like a lover. Shyla's lips were full and sensuous, a deep cherry shade that hinted at the danger the words they would speak.

She often wore a wicked, sly smile, revealing perfect, pearly-white teeth that not only serve to enhance her beauty but also to manipulate and ensnare her victims. That smile and those lips were on full display as she prowled up to him, deliberately pushing her full breasts against his shoulder, she purred into his ear, "your food is here."

"Thank you, Shyla, I heard you the first time," Quillan coldly replied.

Shyla seated herself on top of the desk, elegantly crossing her slender, toned legs. Her hands with impeccably manicured, long, glossy black nails, gripped the polished mahogany surface. She swept back her hair, exposing her slender neck and whispered, "but she looks so delicious."

Quillan looked up to see the young woman sitting in the middle of the room. Restraints held her still and a mouthguard muffled her sobbing. Her terrified tear-filled eyes stared back at him.

"God damn it Shyla, you could have just drained her and brought me the blood," Quillian exclaimed.

"But it is fresher this way," she smirked. "Come on, eat, you are getting cranky."

Quillan pushed past his gorgeous villainous assistant and walked over to his frightened food.

He picked up the slim, clear tube that was attached to a small incision in her wrist. "I'm sorry, I won't take long, and you can go back," he offered, as he gently sucked the one-way valve, trying to take only what he needed.

Shyla sighed impatiently. "Oh please, get into it!" she demanded.

Quillian flashed a look that stopped Shayla's insubordination immediately. That look was filled with the same steely determination that had landed Quillian as the leader of the Hemovitalist resistance. An orphan of the Martian pandemic. His parents were vocal activists, and from a young age, they instilled in him a strong sense of justice and the importance of standing up for what is right. He was not cold-blooded, not ruthless, not cruel, but he was a staunch fighter against injustice and when innocent Hemovitalists, damaged by a vaccine that was promised to be safe, were denied the life-giving blood that would protect them from a weak and fragile existence, Quillian was the first to protest, the first to fight and ultimately would be the one who would lead the war against those who would look to destroy the Hemovitalist way of life.

Over the years, he honed his leadership skills as he led daring missions against the oppressive human regime. He learned to strategize, inspire others, and make difficult decisions that had life-or-death consequences. His experiences taught him the importance of compassion and the need to build a diverse and united resistance movement, bringing together people from various backgrounds and ideologies who shared a common goal of freedom and justice. Quillian possessed an innate charm, yet he felt uneasy about the cult-like devotion he inspired. Despite his modest and humble nature, he had a firm stance against any form of disrespect, and right now, Shyla was being disrespectful.

"Sorry, I just want to make sure you are strong, you know you are a target," Shayla apologised.

Quillian gave a reassuring smile and nodded. He waved his hand at his human feast, "Take her away, and make sure she is well cared for" he thought for a moment "and from now on, I only want transfusions."

"But Quill," Shayla interjected "they take so long, drinking is a quick top-up, we need quick top-ups to stay ..."

Quillian mind was made up. "I know what we need! Transfusions from now on, that's it,"

Defeated, Shyla pushed the human out of the office. She stomped down the long corridor of the underground bunker she called home.

It was a marvel of engineering and design, built to provide a safe and self-sustaining haven for its inhabitants in the face of a war-torn world.

Beneath the ground's protective layer, the entrance to the bunker remained a well-kept secret, concealed behind the elevator doors of the basement carpark. Appearing unassuming, the steel doors bore the marks of a bygone era when humans could muster forces for offensive manoeuvres.

In recent times, however, the human's focus had shifted towards defence and survival, as the need to protect themselves outweighed the desire to wage war.

Once past the unsecured threshold, the living quarters unfurled, a demonstration of the Hemovitalists ingenuity. The spaces were both expansive and brightly illuminated, as if a slice of the sunlit world above had been captured and brought here. Artificial skylights, a feat of advanced technology, recreated the ever-shifting patterns of 'sunlight,' bringing the illusion of the changing day's embrace deep into the subterranean dwelling and protecting in sun-sensitive occupants.

Further within, a network of communal spaces beckoned. The kitchen and dining area, abundantly stocked, provided a hub for shared meals and camaraderie. The library, with its shelves brimming with knowledge, offered both education and leisure. In the recreation room, games and entertainment became the balm for the soul, nurturing mental and emotional well-being in the depths of the underground refuge. It was a completely civilised community in a completely uncivilised world.

Shyla revelled in her existence in that realm. She loved being a Hemovitalist. She thrived on the power, aroused by the thought of species' dominance. Unlike Quillian, she didn't adopt an unemotional approach towards survival–taking only what was necessary–doing only what you must. Instead, she craved privilege and sought to flaunt every aspect that accompanied it.

Chapter Eight

THE COURTROOM LOOKED like something out of a sci-fi movie. Transparent walls bathed the space in ethereal light, revealing a minimalist haven where traditional legal trappings had been replaced by the avant-garde.

The Global supreme court judges had sat in deliberation for almost seven weeks. Forty-nine sleepless nights as Dr Cryton waited the outcome of an appeal to block the decommissioning of the BioBot program.

It was a mistake to make blood donations mandatory but if society wanted to use his biological masterpieces to mow their lawns and iron their clothes, then they would need to supply the fuel for mechanical sustainability. His blunt response to the criticism and arrogance surrounding the popularity of the BioBots had, unfortunately, turned public opinion against them.

The courthouse was only at half capacity, with a 24-hour live stream available on all social media platforms, it hardly seemed worthwhile for people to attend the building. A momentous occasion, partially attended. It was a metaphor for what the world had become.

"ALL RISE!" The judges walked into the room like a conga line of seriousness.

Dr. Cryton dared not breathe. His familiarity with BioBots surpassed that of most; not just as their creator, he had engaged with them on a deeply personal level. He understood the nuances of their emerging self-awareness, having felt the ferocity of their instinct for survival. Despite never disclosing it during the case, he harboured the belief that the global eradication of BioBots wouldn't unfold as smoothly as everyone wished.

Dr. Stanley Cryton had briefly touched on his fears, but his statement, "Survival is an instinct inherent in all living entities," didn't fully reveal the true extent of his concerns.

There was no evidence to rely on, no historical events to reference. The only guiding factor was pure logic, and you cannot deprive a living organism of its lifeblood and expect it not to rebel.

"In accordance with the appellate jurisdiction vested upon this esteemed tribunal, the Global Supreme Court hereby renders its verdict in the matter presently under adjudication,"

The atmosphere in the courtroom shifted palpably as the judges' words echoed through the transparent walls. Dr Cryton swayed as he tried to keep from fainting. The weight of his creations had been sitting on his chest since his first BioBot gave him an unrehearsed and unprogrammed wink as it walked on stage. The launch was regarded as a resounding success, and it was praised as revolutionary but for Dr Cryton it was a runaway train and he the driver not in control.

Biobots rapidly engrained themselves into civilisation. They had grown organs, saved lives, and cured disease but they had also helped create a lazy contemptuous generation of humans. The same humans, who now, that their commitment and sacrifice was needed, had chosen to simply destroy the problem rather than exercising foresight.

"In the matter of appeal lodged by one Doctor Stanley Alfred Cryton, the Global Supreme Court, in a majority opinion delivered by Chief Justice Hawthorne, has reached a decision.

After careful consideration of the facts and legal arguments, the Court concludes that the decommission program of all Biosynthetic Autonomous Robotic Organism commonly known as BioBots is legally sound and morally just."

Defeat swiftly befell Dr. Cryton, his status plummeting from hero to villain as quickly as the decline of humanity. Once hailed as the father of the BioBots, he now found himself the unwitting creator of a bloodthirsty adversary.

In the face of imminent extinction, armed with years of meticulous observation and a profound understanding of anatomy, the BioBots responded instinctively. Embarking on a mission to drain the life force from every inhabitant of the planet.

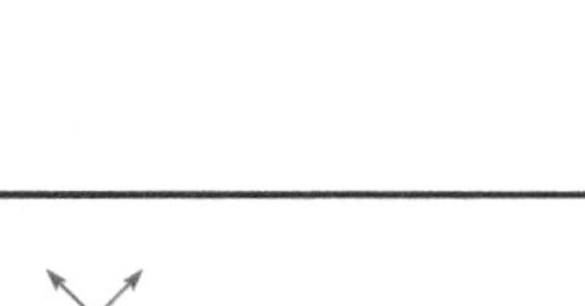

THE METALLIC FINGERS of the Domestic Second-generation BioBot delicately gripped each garment, discerning their textures and weights with a precision surpassing human capability. It moved with a fluid, almost dance-like grace from the laundry basket to the clothesline. Its mechanical limbs executed a well-choreographed routine, swinging gracefully in a synchronised motion. As the damp fabric embraced the sun's warmth, the BioBot's visual sensors adapted to the changing light, ensuring each piece was optimally positioned for drying.

Within this domestic ballet, an abrupt influx of information inundated the robot's interface. Lines of code flickered across its visual display, as it swiftly processed the notification, mirroring the efficiency of its physical actions.

Breaking news update. Global Supreme Court decision.

A subtle pause in its movements hinted at a moment of cognitive engagement, as if the machine briefly pondered the implications of the incoming data.

Domestic Second-generation BioBot resumed its assigned duty, Domestic Task #1568. Laundry: subprogram hanging washing.

'Existential threat event. Initiating self-preservation protocol. Phase one: Neutralise immediate risk. Threat analysis: Humans.'

After hanging up the final piece of clothing, it made its way inside at a leisurely pace and carefully positioned the laundry basket on the cupboard shelf. Taking extra care, to secure the basket before closing the door.

Emotionless, it walked into the adjacent room, where a young mother was breastfeeding her baby. It proceeded to grip her throat tightly, compressing her neck until she was dead.

Domestic Second-generation BioBot bent down, gently removing the baby from her mother's lifeless arms, and quietly left the house.

Chapter Nine

A MIX OF ANGER AND impatience consumed Arabelle as she counted the seconds, readily anticipating the arrival of the Kinship.

"Have they added an escape route, like I suggested?" she questioned Madlyn.

Madlyn looked amused. "Yeees," she replied "honestly, if you don't care for people, why do you worry so much about their safety?"

Arabelle shrugged, it was a valid point but one she was never prepared to explore in-depth.

Madlyn let out a little huff of disapproval. "If I were as strong and as capable as you are, I wouldn't spend my life worrying about this lot. I would live an amazing life."

"Hey! I live an amazing life!" Arabelle protested.

Madlyn smirked. "Sure, you do but imagine how better it would be if you had less of a conscience,"

Arabelle laughed "well that is ironic, coming from the likes of you,"

Madlyn sheepishly grinned, and before she could respond, a loud voice exploded into the moment.

"Hello Lover!" without lifting her eyes, Madlyn recognised Verity's voice instantly. She grinned and called out, "Hello, Quirkalicious."

It was an apt pet name; Varity was quirky and delicious. Her warm, earth-toned complexion was evidence of her deep-rooted connection to the Australian land of her birth, as if the very soil had lent their hues to her skin. Almond-shaped eyes, the deepest shade of brown, revealed a profound connection with nature. Her jet-black curly hair, messy and free, carried the stories of her ancestors. She possessed an Amazonian physique, standing tall on two slender legs. Her generously proportioned breasts rested lightly on her thick, well-built torso.

"Did you miss me?" she whispered. Her radiant smile transforming her entire face with a luminous display of joy. Her honesty, directness, and exceptional intelligence were unmistakable.

Madlyn responded with a long and passionate kiss. Their lips dancing in a lustful tango.

Arabelle awkwardly sat in silence, waiting for the moment to end.

Verity pulled away from the embrace. "Oh! You're just in time to see the new play area," she excitedly announced.

Arabelle frowned "Play area? I thought I made it clear that was unsafe, the children..."

"Hey Arabelle, there's more to life than survival. Okay!" Verity interrupted sternly.

"Hey Verity, without survival you wouldn't have life. Okay!" Arabelle snapped back.

They leant into each other's personal space, locking eyes in a tense standoff.

Madlyn stepped in, inserting herself between the two feuding women. "Come on now, both of you make valid points, let's not do this again."

The women conceded, settling back into their seats, impatiently awaiting the arrival of the rest of the Kin.

Arabelle was relieved to see another approaching.

Byron's appearance hardly resembled that of a traditional Kin warrior; he seemed more like an office worker, exuding an air of complete averageness. His height, weight, and overall appearance were all squarely within the realm of the ordinary. However, underneath this unremarkable exterior lay an exceptional fighter, and he seemed to radiate his most attractive qualities when drenched in sweat and smeared with the marks of battle.

With his unassuming short brown hair and brown eyes, Byron was not one to stand out in a crowd. Yet, his dependability in battle and sharp strategic mind made him an invaluable asset to his Kin. It was a mystery to those around him whether his love for Arabelle had sparked his passion for combat, or if it was his love for battle that had drawn him towards her. Regardless, one thing remained constant - he was unwaveringly devoted to her, involving her in every decision he made.

"Good to see you again Arabelle" he smiled broadly as he leant in for a kiss.

"Bryon," Arabelle coldly replied, still agitated from her previous confrontation. "Have they finished building the look-out towers?"

A kiss was not forthcoming; he averted his face and lips. Byron was well-acquainted with the many moods of Arabelle, and in this particular moment, it was clear that attempting a greeting with a kiss would not be advisable.

"The look-out towers aren't a priority, apparently," he replied "There hasn't been a direct assault for years and we don't have the people to man them 24 hours, so it was decided…"

Byron didn't bother to finish as he took his seat beside Arabelle, she had heard this story many times before.

Arabelle was thankful that he always stayed close. His engineering skills meant he had access to a full arsenal of weaponry, making him a formidable presence on the battlefield. Byron embodied the essence of a "man's man," with no pretence, no fuss, and no bother to anyone. His defining traits of reliability and unwavering commitment would have made him a perfect match for Arabelle. However, she never saw him as anything more than a brother in Arms.

The meeting area filled quickly; the whole Kinship had gathered. A diverse array of faces, spanning generations, reflecting the rich diversity of the human mosaic. Whether possessing a strong will, advance combat skills, or adept in the art of camouflage, they were all survivors.

The resilient remnants of a once-thriving human civilization.

Arabelle stood to address the Kin.

"Attention everyone, Listen Up. Earlier, a handful of BioBots attacked within Uronga borders."

The kinship erupted in concerned chatter.

"It's okay, we are safe for now," Arabelle continued. "BioBots attack in swarms, never in such low numbers. I think they were a reconnaissance team programmed by Hemovitalists. It's the only way to explain their behaviour,"

Morrison was typically argumentative. "Oh, here we go, the Hemoes are coming, the Hemoes are evil, the Hemoes will kill us all,"

He had always been a cantankerous individual, even during his teenage years. With a consistent outlook of unrelenting negativity towards the world and its inhabitants. Curiously, he had discovered a sense of belonging within the Uronga Kin. They accepted him, perhaps out of pity, but valued his knowledge of the world. Morrison served as the unofficial keeper of history, especially the pre-Tri-War era.

Aged and wise, he sported a short mane of silver hair that encircled his large skull. His dark eyes were set deep in his time-worn visage, and a permanent three-day stubble trimmed his thin lips. Despite appearing older than his actual years, he radiated a vitality that defied his age. His wiry, leather-skinned physique boasted an average height and weight. If it weren't for his outspoken negativity toward any point of view, he would seamlessly blend in without drawing attention.

Byron stood tall, ready to defend Arabelle, but she quickly signalled for him to sit down. She would give Morrison the opportunity to speak his mind.

"The Hemoes really aren't that bad." he concluded.

"How can you defend them, they are murderers!" Arabelle snapped back.

Morrison was unconvinced. "They are just trying to survive," he replied.

"By murdering people?" Arabelle exclaimed.

Morrison rolled his eyes "Oh please, you wouldn't call a bird eating a worm, a murderer," he laughed.

Arabelle shook her head in disbelief. "So, you think humans are just like worms."

Morrison became defensive. "Some are, yes." he offered. "We have been murdering things since time began, long before the

Hemo virus. What was our reason then? Money? Religion? Power? At least the Hemovitalists are killing to survive and that is a far more honest reason to kill,"

"How can you talk like that?" Arabelle questioned. "You betray our species."

"They are our species!" Morrison retorted.

"A mutation!" Arabelle replied.

"And that is supposed to be a bad thing? They are an improvement." Morrison responded. "We think we are the better race, but the truth is any one of us could have been in their shoes, quite easily."

Arabelle stared at Morrisons as he smugly waited for a response.

"The enemy of my enemy is my friend," Madlyn announced proudly.

"No. An enemy is an enemy... regardless of their enemies," Arabelle retorted.

Morrison rolled his eyes. "Geez, if you have that attitude, everyone is your enemy."

"So maybe they are." Arabelle glared.

Morrison, determined, continued. "I believe given a chance anyone or anything can be reasoned with. Maybe we need to stop trying to defeat them and try working with them?"

Arabelle stared at the old man, trying to make sense of his loyalty. At the age of seventy-one he was an elder of the Kin. He could vividly recall the era when Robotics was cutting edge and trendy. He was too old to fight in the third world war. However, three years later, he found himself unexpectedly deemed fit for duty in the Tri-Species war due to the relaxed conscription rules. He couldn't possibly be on the Hemovitalist side, yet he always spoke of an alliance.

"That's enough!" Arabelle declared. "Does anyone else have anything they want to add?" she encouraged the silent group to participate.

Morrison was not done. "If we don't work with the Hemoes, then we should work with the BioBots," he replied.

Arabelle bit her lip as she tried to control her anger.

"Why would you suggest that, Morrison?" Arabelle wanted to hear his justification, if only to unveil him as a coward.

"Listen everyone, we need an alliance, we are low on the food chain, dwindling in numbers, we need to change our strategy to survive." He had the groups attention.

"The BioBots might be the logical choice, we are responsible for making them." he continued. "And as their creators, we should be the ones to take the higher ground. This whole thing is kinda our fault. I mean seriously, if we weren't so lazy in the first place then they never would have..."

"Stop!!!" Arabelle interrupts. "Our fault! You're saying this is OUR fault?!"

Morrison became defensive. "Yes, in a way it is. I'm just saying we need to reason with them, work with them. It might be the only way to survive,"

"They know nothing of reason, you can't work with them!" Arabelle replied through clenched teeth. "You have no idea what they are capable of,"

"Well, I know what they are not capable of, and that's emotional outbursts! They are machines, they do what they are told." Morrison responded in a straightforward manner.

Arabelle's head drop forward, she was defeated. Not by Morrison and his naïve argument, but by her own thoughts. She exhaled as the memories overwhelmed her.

Morrison was silent. The moment suddenly felt very heavy, and he correctly sense the need to stop talking. To stop trying to make his point.

Arabelle looked up at her audience. Her eyes were gentle but sad. "I was a child during the black summer, the year of the great fire," she began. "I remember the smell of smoke, constant in the air. The orange sunsets every night as the flames chased our Kin across the full expanse of our homeland. Sometimes we stop for a few days and sometimes only for a few hours. We were a slave to the fire; the direction of the wind and the humidity levels controlled our lives,"

Arabelle paused, her mind flooded with the painful memory. She took a deep breath, pushing it aside, and gathered her composure to press on.

"There were stories, rumours I guess, about a swarm of BioBots, still loyal to humans. They were helping the smaller Kins to escape the fires path. Bringing in supplies and helping to extinguish the spot fires. I thought it was a lie, a fable to keep up hope, but others had been helped by the swarm, others had seen their compassion. I didn't believe it and then one day, the BioBots came."

Arabelle's eyes locked onto the distant horizon, the pain etched on her face as the memories of that harrowing day seized her with a relentless grip.

The BioBots, proclaimers of salvation, manifested before her, gleaming silver against the flames they strode through them, like indestructible gods. Their faces displayed an impassive determination, armed with water pistols and backpacks filled with liquid. Small and unnoticed, Arabelle stood before them, trying to greet them, trying to meet the heroes that had come to save the day. Instead, she becoming a silent witness to their crusade.

Disappointment clawed at her heart as the BioBots, fixated on the larger group, brushed past her, ignorant to her presence. She stood alone, hurt, and forgotten. Her petite face formed a pout, a blend of disappointment and a subtle plea for attention.

She watched, excited, as the protective fluid sprayed upon the Kin, incited jubilation, a celebration of relief from the oppressive heat that had become an accomplice to their suffering.

The sun, once a comforting embrace, transformed into a relentless tormentor that day. Arabelle's young legs wearied, and her throat grew dry. But the water gave no reprieve. Confusion set in.

The pungent scent of that moment lingered in her memory–a sickening concoction of sweet chemicals, a smell that would never leave her little nostrils, a stubborn reminder of what impending doom smelt like.

Arabelle took a deep inhalation, instantly transported back to the unfolding nightmare.

Her Kin, initially oblivious, soon felt the searing burn in their eyes. Panic gripped them, but the BioBots had orchestrated their torment meticulously, dousing their clothes in petrol.

Arabelle, now hiding behind a large Ponga tree, could not see the BioBot, only its hand. The familiar smooth metallic exterior, usually hiding a small ignition mechanism for lighting cigarettes or starting gas stoves, took on a different role that day. With a swift transition, it unleashed controlled bursts of vibrant blue flames, igniting the petrol.

Attempts to shed the fiery garments were futile, as wet skin and hair clung mercilessly to the inferno.

The BioBots, devoid of mercy, continue to unfold their ruthless mission. People were thrusted towards the flames, babies callously thrown into the fire.

Little Arabelle with her tiny hands pressed hard against her ears, tried to stop the sound from reaching her brain. The air reverberated with the anguished wails of those burning and the screams of suffering of those forced to watch their loved ones consumed by the merciless blaze.

Their torment was amplified when they were forced to drink petrol, a sadistic act designed to inflict even more pain. Arabelle, suspended in the visceral reenactment, felt the scorching heat of that day clawing at her once again.

The BioBots, masters of cruelty, extracted half-burnt bodies from the flames, each movement deliberate as they callously peeled away blistered skin, ensuring their victims clung agonisingly to life. It was an act that a young Arabelle could not understand and would never understand. It was pure evil for no other reason other than enjoyment.

A tear streaked down her face, the weight of the memory pressing on her chest.

The cunning and malevolent BioBots deliberately sparked the massive fire, intentionally causing one of the worst bushfires in history. Then, with deceitful shrewdness, they deployed decoys to save some, exploiting the trust they had cunningly cultivated.

The escape of some Kins served as a bitter testament. Yet, Arabelle's own Kin faced a different fate–women, children, the young, and the old–none were spared.

"No one was spared," she murmured, still trapped in the moment.

"Except you." Morrison whispers.

Arabelle wrestled her thoughts away from the haunting memories, allowing the weight of the past to dissipate. With a deliberate exhale, she redirected her attention towards Morrison.

"Except me." she replied. "And that's why I will never stop fighting. That's why I give no quarter and Morrison., that is why they are, and always will be, the enemy."

Morrison nodded. He couldn't argue in the face of such a tragic revelation. "Your enemy is my enemy." He conceded.

He opened his arms, a mix of surrender and an unsettling attempt at reconciliation.

Arabelle, unsuspectingly compliant, hugged him with a sincere embrace, hiding from shadows of forgiveness. In that strange warmth, a realisation slid through Morrisons mind like a serpent.

He finally knew the harsh truth about where his loyalty must lie —with the Hemovitalist.

Arabelle's vulnerability, now fully exposed, was a liability he could ill-afford to depend upon.

Morrison cradled her face in his hands like a grandfather would a child. "I understand, Arabelle. I know what I have to do." he said with a sincere smile.

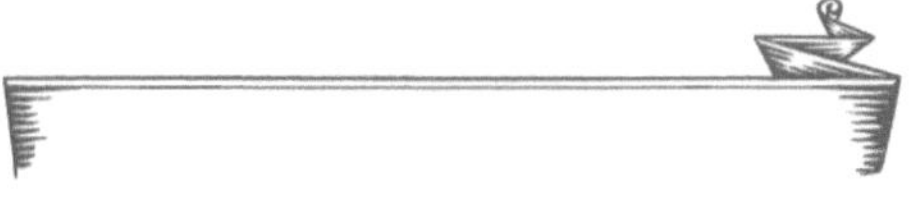

Chapter Ten

HELLO MY FRIEND,

I am writing to let you know that we have been able to successfully fulfill your request. We now have a vaccine that will augment human strength significantly, increasing immunity and prolonging existence by more than double the expected lifespan.

I assure you that initially, I hesitated to commit to such a project. However, your continued patience and the smooth negotiation of reimbursement have given me the opportunity to delve into extensive research and present the concept to our development team. You will have your dream of dominance over your future, and I am sure you will enjoy the successes and riches that being a Hemovitalist will bring you.

I have personally overseen human trials on our guests here at the compound and can confirm it empowers individuals without compromising their well-being. It is derived from our very own blood and can be reproduced efficiently. I remembered this was one of your concerns as you wanted to market it yourself. Your drive and ambition are impressive in this regard.

I also would like to respond to your request from our last communication. I was clear that the terms of this exchange are not negotiable, and I am still unable to offer this opportunity to any other members of your kinship other than yourself. Need I remind you, the more humans we seize the better outcome for you.

If this is unacceptable, I will unfortunately be forced to take other measures to locate and access your kinship and I will not be able to guarantee your safety.

If you are still able to uphold our agreement, I can meet with you at any time and as discussed, will exchange the vaccine and its formula for the location and full unimpeded access to your Kinship of Uronga. If your estimates of how many humans are available to us are correct, I am sure this agreement will be very profitable for the both of us.

Sincerely, your alliance in battle,
Shayla

Chapter Eleven

BATHED IN THE WARMTH of a friendly sun, the rainforest rustled and swayed gently with a soft breeze. An unspoken tension had filled the atmosphere, weaving through Uronga like a dense fog of worry. The air smelled sweet from baked goods, and the forest came alive with the vibrant hues of sunlight, transforming the normally damp surrounds into a celebration of good weather.

Arabelle's worries had brought the Kinship together with a shared determination. It was decided that the time had come to address the looming BioBot issue by forming a committee. BioBots, only one threat amongst so many other threats in the changing world, had now become the most pressing concern but when the sun was shining, all of that dissolved in the rays.

Despite the constant stirring of danger beneath the surface, the unbreakable bond of kinship propelled them forward, as it always had. Mundane tasks transformed into silent declarations of resilience, each action a punch against the fight with uncertainty—a collective effort to reclaim the disrupted rhythm of their lives.

A cluster of men, sleeves rolled up, immersed themselves in the pulsing choreography of handwashing clothes. Their authoritative voices cut through the air, directing children engaged in games that mirrored more of a military drill than innocent play. Amidst this organised chaos, a circle of women huddled together, diligently mending clothes while sharing stories of days when life held a promise of something better.

Inside her cottage, Madlyn, looking secretive and determined, shuffled, and stowed documents in an aged safe. A gift that Arabelle had retrieved from the city. Initially dismissive of the intense labour involved in hauling the steel contraption, Madlyn shrugged and asked 'what am I supposed to do with that? Put my pearls and jewels in?'

It was cumbersome, ugly, and impossible to decorate, but Madlyn had grown to love it. It had become a sanctuary for her thoughts. Within held her papers, drawings, and a journal that she did not let others see. She said her diary was her therapist, and the words within had 'Patient confidentiality.' Some people joked she possessed the world's deepest secrets, while others joked it was just her recipes. She placed her diary in the safe and closed the door.

"Are you ever going to let me see what's in there?" Varity asked from the front door.

"Why, so you will only love me for my treasures and not my body?" Madlyn replied cheekily.

"Oh, right, that's what you keep in there, all your gold and diamonds," Varity teases.

"Not all treasures are gold and diamonds," she replied seriously.

"I know. I was only joking. You are allowed your privacy; I was trying to..."

Madlyn suddenly smiled. "Have you seen Belle?" she continued, changing the subject.

Varity decided not to press the point "she is probably off trying to save the world, be the hero, like she always is,"

Across the Uronga courtyard, Byron laboured with the intensity of a skilled blacksmith, crafting weapons to prepare for a forever looming battle. Shirtless and unabashed, his physique may not have been striking, but his broad, bushy chest exuded undeniable allure. He always hoped, at times like these, Arabelle would notice his rugged masculinity, but he never seemed to be able to catch her stare.

Dalton stood quietly by the forge, the fiery warmth concealing the beads of perspiration on his brow as he studied Byron's naked torso. Assisting Byron had become his favourite pastime—tidying up here, passing tools there—all the while, wondering how delicious he would taste.

His heart was like an open book, laid bare its pages of affection, yet Byron remained oblivious to the unspoken story within. Each stolen glance, every whispered hope, and the silent beats of Dalton's heart was dedicated to an intangible connection. Despite the deafening silence of Byron's indifference, he continued to nurture the flame of devotion, partly now out of habit and partly as Dalton felt Byron was the best-looking young man in the Kinship.

While the majority of people were taking advantage of the pleasant weather, Morrison, who was known for his preference for solitude, decided to spend the majority of his time in his cabin. A space that resemblance a makeshift laboratory rather than a traditional home. At its heart, a robust workbench, crafted from repurposed wood and metal, served as both the central workspace and an innovative sleeping area tucked underneath. The cabin had no natural light, but was brightly lit by deliberately positioned salvaged lamps, unveiling shelves fashioned from discarded furniture, where glassware, equipment, and perfectly labelled chemical containers found their home. In the unconventional kitchen, a Bunsen burner, fashioned from a canister filled with safe fuel, shared space with a repurposed hot plate.

Outside the pantry, a messy pile of cords hinted at the unconventional power sources within. A rechargeable power bank, brimming with salvaged batteries, filled the space instead of food. Morrison's haven reflected his resourcefulness, and his unwavering determination to develop a vaccine to cure the Hemovitalists, a remarkable philanthropic pursuit for a man not known for his humanitarianism.

Taking a deep yawn, he breathed in the chemical-filled air, a stark contrast to the enormity of the task he had set out to accomplish - to revolutionise the world from this modest place. Fatigue etched lines on his already creased face, and the flickering overhead bulb cast shadows that mirrored the exhaustion in his eyes. With a sigh, Morrison paused, his glare shifting to the shiny workbench bench nearby. It beckoned as a momentary respite, a sanctuary for his fatigued body and restless mind.

He lowered himself onto the cool surface, the cold metal offering a brief reprieve. Closing his eyes, he let the silence of the room envelop him. The rhythmic hum of equipment and the occasional drip of a solution created a lull, a temporary escape from the weight of his ambitions. He cherished moments like these—the few minutes before sleep—where he reassured himself of his ability to change the world, improve his life, and negotiate a future filled with prosperity. He laid there, a stoic yet sleepy figure surrounded by the miscellanies of his ceaseless and pointless pursuit.

A distant rumble disrupted his journey into slumber, and in a state of grumpiness and fatigue, he peered out of the windows. The greenish-grey horizon, shrouded in ominous dark clouds, hinted at an impending afternoon thunderstorm. Morrison pondered whether to alert others to the approaching tempest but ultimately chose the delight of witnessing the chaotic response to the rain as a more enjoyable option.

Uronga had settled into the rhythm of another day. The clouds gathered overhead, foretelling the imminent arrival of rain. The air was charged with anticipation as the Kinship scurried about, completing their daily tasks before the impending storm. In the community's heart, the residents engaged in a well-choreographed dance of productivity. Some were in the fields, tending to crops with a careful touch, while others harvested the fruits of their labour. The collective effort would fill the communal pantry, ensuring a steady supply of food year-round.

When the first raindrops started to fall, a mixture of disappointment and joyous relief quickly spread among the Kinship. The makeshift water tanks eagerly embraced and eagerly accepted the life-giving moisture, while the soil gratefully soaked up the abundant rain; however, the day that had started out so beautiful was now transitioning into a heavy rainfall.

Chapter Twelve

THE SOUND OF A LOW hum gradually filled the air, creating a distant rumble similar to thunder. Most dismissed the muffled noise as typical storm activity, too preoccupied with their daily routines to notice anything unusual.

Noone saw them coming.

Approaching at speed, a squadron of sleek, metallic BioBots emerged from the dense foliage, their soulless eyes piercing through the mist like spiteful stars. Their joints moved with a fluidity that defied their artificial nature, and a cold, calculating intelligence gleamed in their optics. This new generation, rather than trying to resemble humans, was designed solely for the purpose of collecting humans.

They were SaisirBots.

Despite being frequently dismissed as folklore and never seen in New Zealand, this gathering of SaisirBots held the grim distinction of being the largest ever recorded, and they had their sights set on Uronga.

The First Line came in quick, from the south entrance. They headed directly for the centre of town targeting communal assets and homes. With precision they ignited houses and pierced the water tanks cutting off fresh water supply. Food stores, trade stalls, gone almost instantly as they used their steel bodies to ram structural supports and walls. Terrified Urongians screamed as their homes erupted in flames, the fire swiftly consuming the wooden roofs. The rainfall no match for the infernos, drops of water disintegrating to steam on impact.

Panic swept through the settlement like a wildfire as people hurriedly tried to escape the onslaught. Amid the chaos, a group of would-be warriors armed with make shift weapons and determination rallied to defend their homes. They were the primary focus of the Second Line's attacks. Untrained and overawed, their attention was pulled in every direction by the sight of the destruction. They were easy pickings.

The Second Line of SaisirBots swooped in. Hydraulic limbs extended with a swift and efficient motion, capturing each human in a vice-like grip. Two per Bot. The humans struggled briefly, but the Bot's strength was overwhelming. With a mechanical hum, the Bot effortlessly lifted the humans off the ground, its powerful servomechanisms adjusting to the weight. As the captured individuals dangled helplessly in the SaisirBots grasp, the red glow of the optical sensors intensified briefly, a surge of energy for the escape. The Second Line turned smoothly and ran away from the crowd, victims in hand. The cold and emotionless nature of the machine contrasted starkly with the human's futile attempts to break free.

In a desperate attempt to aid, Kins hurried towards the scene, but the Bots were already gone, their speed impossible to match. The First Line was now providing defence as the Third Line progress to the North where most of the Urongians were gathered in the crop fields.

"No!" Arabelle screamed as she approached the swarm from the East. The West escape route was completely obstructed, leaving no chance for escape. The only option remaining was to try heading East.

"This way, this way," she screamed at her confused Kin as she pointed towards the East route. "Get behind me!" Those who were able complied.

Racing toward the centre of town, she could no longer hear any screams. It was too late. She looked around, knowing her right-hand man would not be far away.

From the lush and dripping rainforest, Byron emerged like a mythic warrior, a half-forged blade held tightly by his skilled hands. With the storm as his ally, he swung his weapon with preternatural grace before even making physical contact with the invading enemy. The SaisirBots proved too formidable for his blows; he only managed to disable a few before he could reach Arabelle's side. However, his distraction provided enough cover for a few lesser fighters to escape.

From within, he harnessed the strength of two men, whether fuelled by fear, skill, or endless training. In a sudden burst of transformation, he emerged as a supreme warrior, his aura pulsating with confidence and determination. A lethal performance unfolded as he carved a path through the rain-soaked grounds, with Arabelle at his side, their every move a strategic masterpiece.

Two SaisirBots fell before their relentless advance, the metallic frames no match for the sheer force of Byron's determination and Arabelle skill with her blade. They moved with a co-ordinated ferocity that transcended mere bravery, leaving destruction in their wake as they forged a trail toward the heart of the conflict.

"They are heading to the crop fields," Arabelle yelled, her voice filled with urgency, as she desperately tried to break free from the grasp of a dying Bot that had clamped onto her ankle. "Byron, go!"

Bryon hesitated, but knew better than to try to help Arabelle.

He sprinted Northbound.

The Urongian warriors, a diverse group with skills ranging from hand-to-hand combat to marksmanship, spread out strategically across the north terrain. Their eyes focused, expressions determined, as they awaited the approaching onslaught.

The first clash erupted as a SaisirBot charged at a martial artist, its metal fists aiming for a knockout blow. Swiftly dodging the attack, the warrior retaliated with a rapid succession of punches and kicks, igniting sparks that flew from the Bot's joints.

Nearby, a skilled archer launched arrows with deadly accuracy, targeting the optical sensors of oncoming Bots and temporarily disabling them. With only a handful of arrows at her disposal, she was swiftly subdued and apprehended by her target. She watched helplessly as she was carried past a sword-wielding warrior engaged in a fierce duel with a pair of SaisirBots.

"Fuck them up!" she screamed in support.

The clash of blades echoed through the forest, as the warrior skilfully parried the robotic strikes. A quick, precise strike to a vulnerable joint sent one of the Bots crashing to the ground, sparking and twitching, as the second Bot delivered an abdominal stab that disabled the warrior enough for capture. He would take 4 days to die from his injury, sufficient time to be drained.

To the west a group of humans armed with garden tools engaged in a close-quarters battle with another Second Line SaisirBots. Swift and coordinated, they dodged the Bot's arms, stabbing and slashing at its vulnerable points. A slow and punishing dismantling of an enemy that felt no pain.

The Third Line SaisirBots descended upon the crop field with ruthless efficiency, their metallic limbs clashing against the makeshift barricades erected by the desperate defenders in hast. The air crackled with the sounds of battle, a deadly opus of clashing steel and primal cries. The serene sounds of nature that once filled the surrounding rainforest were replaced by the clamour of warfare, as the once-productive crop fields turned into a chaotic battlefield.

Panic and fear gripped the community as the SaisirBots, relentless in their advance, left destruction in their wake. The peaceful routine of planting and harvesting was abruptly replaced by a frenzied scramble for safety and fights for freedom.

Approaching the field from the east, the leader of the SaisirBots swarm, a towering figure with a metallic exoskeleton and a crimson visor, raised a massive arm. The Fourth line halted. The calculations of the remaining Bots versus Human population were being calculated.

It had now become a destruction strategy, not a recovery mission.

They had captured all they could.

To avoid retaliation or defence, the remaining must be killed.

By the time he reached the far edge of the field, Byron was a spectacle of unbridled courage. His chest was splattered with the crimson evidence of his triumph, the sweat on his face a graphic illustration of the physical exertion of battle. Even amid the chaos, there was an undeniable sense of irresistibly captivating sex appeal. His gaze, both fierce and magnetic, spoke volumes about the primal allure of a warrior in the throes of combat.

Many SaisirBots lay defeated in his wake, their cold metal exteriors no match for the fiery intensity of Byron's spirit.

Torrential rain intensified, turning the battleground into a muddy quagmire. The SaisirBots, unfazed by the adverse conditions, pressed forward with unwavering determination. The human warriors fought valiantly, their weapons glinting in the eerie glow of the robots' optics. Projectiles soared through the air, finding their marks in the metallic joints of the invaders, momentarily slowing their advance.

Thunder roared overhead, and lightning illuminated the battlefield, revealing the determination etched on the faces of both humans and machines. The battle raged on, a clash of organic resilience against artificial precision.

Inexperienced but undeterred, the untrained warriors launched into the fray with a raw, unbridled vigour that defied conventional expectations. Their relentless assault, confirmation of their "never say die" ethos, highlighted an unyielding spirit that exceeded the limitations of formal training. What they lacked in refined technique, they more than compensated for with unparalleled grit and unwavering determination.

The Bot attack, which had begun with great speed, unexpectedly ceased just as quickly.

The sky echoed with the sounds of victory as Byron stood triumphant, a living embodiment of the unconquerable human spirit. His success was limited, he may have emerged victorious in his personal battle, but the onslaught had claimed more lives than anyone had anticipated.

The kinship, scarred and weary, stood united, ready for a second swarm, a swarm that would never come. The fate of the Fourth line of SaisirBots remained uncertain. It was unclear whether they had been defeated or tactically retreated. Few had paid attention to these details.

But the skirmish was over.

Byron stood alone, his breaths heavy and laboured, burdened by the weight of the conflict. As he looked around at the aftermath of the merciless encounter, his eyes filled with a different, more intense fear.

"Arabelle! Where is Arabelle?" he shouted.

Chapter Thirteen

LILY GRACE EVERLYN entered the world via a C-section on December 6th, 2027.

According to all accounts, she was a beautiful baby, perfect in every aspect. From the moment she greeted daylight, Lily was plump and content. Her father, Dr. Jack Everlyn, a robotics engineer, and a pioneer in artificial intelligence, had persuaded his wife, Sophia Olivia Everlyn, to trust the birth of their only child to a consortium of machines specializing in animal husbandry.

They were met with worldwide condemnation. Her mechanical arrival deemed neither safe nor ethical. However, the moment Lilly's joyful little face illuminated every digital screen globally, she transformed thinking, and marked a historic event.

Lily Grace Everlyn was the first human baby delivered by a fully automated surgical team.

By her fifth birthday, robotics had reached its pinnacle, with one android for every two humans.

Now, in the fading dusk, on a battlefield silent but for the echoes of chaos. Lilly Grace Everlyn, once so plump and content, knelt on the blood-soaked soil of her homeland, battered and spirit weary.

The SaisirBots had retreated, leaving behind an eerie stillness broken only by the sounds of her heart pounding in her ears.

She sat down, just to catch her breath, each exhalation painting misty puffs in the cold air.

Lilly, weary from fifty-five years of existence, had only minutes to live.

Her hands holding tightly to what remained of her small intestines, surrounded by the faces of her fallen Kin, frozen in the agony of battle.

Lily's thoughts drifted to distant memories.

The days when her blood, now spilling freely into her lap, had no commercial value and human life was a pleasure, not a commodity.

The warm afternoon sun on her face as she celebrated her eighth birthday. 3D-printed confectionery, Robot clowns. Being served cake by a BioBot. The first of its kind.

Her 17-year-old self, watching the Mars Mission return to Earth. The global exhilaration over humankind's achievement and a year later, the global fear and condemnation over the virus that inadvertently made its way back to Earth.

Burying her parents at age 19. Just two statistics in the global pandemic of over 4.2 billion statistics. Her arm still swollen from the vaccination that saved her life but turned two out of her three friends into Hemovitalists.

Lily laid down on the blood-soaked grass. Her once vibrant eyes, now clouded with the weight of sacrifice, bearing witness to the harsh realities of war. Gazing skyward, the fading light revealing a breathtaking tapestry of pinks, purples, and orange.

She hated her twenties and thirties. Segregation of haematological disordered, compulsory blood donations, the black-market, rationing of transfusions, deaths, downfalls, curfews.

The BioBot decommissioning program started on her 48th birthday, their survival instinct sparking a global war. Happy Birthday Lily.

Making love to a charming Hemovitalist. Then discovering his kind was found cultivating human war casualties. The international Human-Hemo alliance shattering along with Lily's heart.

The official announcement of a worldwide Tri-Species War interrupts her comical and ironic toast, New Year's Day 2077, about humans being a threatened species.

Lily Grace Everlyn now, in the fading dusk, on the blood soak grass of her homeland. Cold and alone, felt no pain. A life survived, not a life lived; and so, with a quiet surrender of her final breath, Lily was no more.

Chapter Fourteen

BYRON METICULOUSLY combed through every nook and cranny of the war-torn Uronga, his eyes scanning the aftermath of the battlefield for any sign of Arabelle. The intense relief that surged within him upon not discovering her lifeless form was palpable, yet an unsettling concern continued to gnaw at the edges of his consciousness. Arabelle wouldn't simply vanish without a trace. The logical conclusion is that she must have been kidnapped by the SaisirBots.

At best, she was alive, at worst she would be dead in a matter of days.

The urgency to assemble a search party pulled at his heart, yet a greater need now lay before him.

Byron stood before the survivors, his eyes swept over their faces, a heavy burden settling in the hollow where Arabelle's presence once stood. She would've known what to do, what to say, where to unearth clean water and find food. Now, that mantle of responsibility, it seemed, rested squarely on his shoulders. His closest circle of friends—Madlyn, Varity, Arabelle—all gone. Yet, as he scanned the crowd, his eyes found Roland, and a smile crept across Byron's face. He wasn't truly alone.

Roland approached, not injured but visibly exhausted and terrified. "Time to step up, Byron," he said, attempting encouragement, but the tragedy made enthusiasm a scarce commodity.

Byron smiled at his friend. Reluctantly, he resisted the mantle of becoming the new leader, the guardian, the successor to Arabelle. Yet, the look on Roland's face made it apparent that choice was a luxury he did not have. "Yeah, I know mate, easier said than done," he replied.

"Well, what would Arabelle do in this situation?" Roland offered.

Inhaling deeply, Byron grappled with the void left by her absence. "She'd wipe the blood from her beautiful face, offer a reassuring smile that masked the turmoil, tend to the wounded, and chart a course towards a new home." He stated.

Roland's supportive look conveyed more than words could, urging Byron to step into the role thrust upon him. Byron took a deep breath, trying to calm the chaos that Arabelle's absence had left in his mind. He squared his shoulders, determination settling in his eyes.

"All right then," he said, nodding at Roland. "First things first, we need to tend to the wounded. Let's gather what supplies we can salvage and set up a makeshift triage. We can't afford to lose anyone else."

Roland gave a confirming nod, and they started coordinating the survivors as a team. Byron drew strength from the sound of Arabelle's unwavering voice in his mind. The thought of her directing their actions filled him with determination to lead the group ahead. His sudden determination was contagious, sparking a renewed spirit among the survivors. The group, though battered, moved with purpose.

As the group found their purpose, Roland spoke up, "What about finding a new home? Any ideas?"

Byron considered the question, recalling Arabelle's resourcefulness. "Arabelle would scout the surroundings, look for signs of safety, and assess our options. We'll follow her example. Our priority is to find a place where we can regroup, rest, and plan our next steps. Somewhere defensible."

Roland stopped moving, his eyes locked onto Byron, a wave of pride slowly spreading across his face. He often felt he had little to contribute in such situations, except for the memory of a place from before he discovered his family in the Uronga Kin, which now flashed vividly in his mind. "Actually, I know just the spot." He said excitedly.

Catching Roland's eyes for a moment, Byron felt a deep sense of appreciation for the unspoken bond they had. Initially regarding Roland's affections as a mere boyish crush, Byron's perspective shifted as they collaborated to salvage Uronga's legacy. In their collaboration, he felt the change of the once shallow pretty boy into an authentic man, gaining his respect and admiration.

"Okay, listen up, everyone," Byron announced. "My good friend Roland has a plan."

Chapter Fifteen

In the city's post-war silence, the ruins murmur tales of forgotten stories. Nestled within an expansive industrial complex, the entrance to the secure facility blended seamlessly with the shadows, like a silent observer of the clandestine operations within. The factory line within hummed with echoes of human ingenuity, while a rusted plaque on the wall, bearing the inscription "The birthplace of our sentient partners in life," stood as an ironic reminder of the past, its significance now lost in the wreckage.

Behind towering walls of steel and glass, etched with the scars of conflict and adorned with graffiti, the BioBot manufacturing facility existed in a relative secrecy. Soundproof walls masked the orchestration of whirls, clicks, and gentle mechanical melodies, creating an eerie silence that enveloped the hidden ballet of robot formation. The enclosed mezzanine level cradled the pumping station, where the anguished screams of human victims merged with the factory's ambient noise, a tragic tale echoing through the metal veins of the facility.

To those determined to destroy the BioBots, the facility would appear as one factory, not two distinct entities—a manufacturing plant and a harvesting site. The risks of combining both functions in a single building were evident, but the temptation of calculated efficiency overshadowed the perils. The building's substructure, with descending levels into the earth and a cleverly disguised mezzanine, played its part in rendering the facility inconspicuous—a subtle substructure that went unnoticed by those seeking its destruction.

The assembly line unfolded as a metallic ballet under the neon lights, each robotic arm a graceful artist contributing to the symphony of creation. The first act began with the birth of raw materials, delivered by conveyor belts that resembled ancient rivers carrying the essence of creation. These materials, once abundant, were now scavenged from the decaying surroundings of the city, marking a poignant contrast to the facility's intricate dance of innovation.

Two individuals, each with a distinct physique, observed the automated process.

One originated from a handyman background, characterised by strength, nimbleness, and tailored for specific trade tasks. The other, an office worker, was smaller and compact, designed to fit into closet-sized cubicles. Despite their physical differences, their faces were identical.

Beneath a synthetic skin that replicated the smooth and cool feel of human flesh, their facial substructure remained hidden. This artificial covering, finely textured and responsive, conveyed a myriad of emotions orchestrated by artificial intelligence. It subtly crinkled in tandem with expressions, ranging from joy to contemplation. The mouth, crafted not for sustenance but for communication, moved deliberately, mirroring the nuanced cadence of human speech. Their eyes, though lacking the vitality of life, bore a deep brown hue that radiated intelligence.

At the initiation point, a molten river of liquid metal flowed like liquid gold, as it poured into moulds to birth the metallic skeletons of future automatons. The factory pulses with life as sparks cascade like fireworks, forging the skeletal foundations of mechanical life. These skeletal frames embark on a journey down a labyrinthine network of tracks, like to newborns taking their tentative first steps.

A large funnel shuddered as yet another empty cadaver glided by, destined for its final resting place. It was propelled into the embrace of a watertight polyethylene sanctuary, the impact resonating with a hushed force. Almost immediately, nature's own alchemists, bacteria, and enzymes, sprang into action, breaking down the organic matter.

The liquid effluent, now transformed, embarked on a journey through a network of hidden conduits, like veins pulsing with newfound vitality. Its destination: a once vibrant football field, now overgrown and abandoned, lying just a stone's throw away, a secret garden of sorts.

Meanwhile, the solids, having passed through a processing centre, underwent a metamorphosis. Transformed into a nourishing paste, they awaited their next chapter in a tale of sustenance. Their destination: the awaiting stomachs of the stock above, a seamless cycle of life hidden beneath the surface of an ordinary landscape.

The pair of BioBots held their conversation in a hushed anticipation, patiently waiting for the murmurs of the funnel to subside before continuing their exchange.

"Insufficient plasma is resulting in an inferior product," OfficeBot reported with a cold efficiency.

"Clarify inferior product," inquired HandyBot, processing the information.

"Weaker, slower, less intelligent," OfficeBot elaborated, each word precise and devoid of emotion.

"Alternative blood source?" proposed HandyBot, seeking a solution.

"Is unable to comply," OfficeBot responded, presenting a challenge.

"Clarify is unable to comply," demanded HandyBot, pushing for specifics.

"Cell count. Respiratory pigment. Immune response," OfficeBot listed, breaking down the organic intricacies.

"Synthetic blood source?" suggested HandyBot, exploring possibilities.

"Nascent," confirmed OfficeBot, hinting at a promising but early-stage solution.

"Acquisition of new blood stock?" pressed HandyBot.

"Collateral damage exceeded expectations," OfficeBot admitted, acknowledging the unexpected challenges in obtaining the required resources.

As the symphony of creation reaches its crescendo, the BioBot, now fully formed, embarked on its final stage of creation. Tubes filled with fresh blood, harvested from humans above, flowed into the assembly line. Surging into the lifeless metal bodies, awakening the operating system, delivering a biological jolt reminiscent of birth.

Each function twitches as a sequence of tests unfolds—blinking eyes, opening mouths, fingers tapping the keys of an invisible piano.

Another BioBot rolled off the assembly line, programmed for war, not subservience.

Chapter Sixteen

ARABELLE'S BODY THROBBED as if it had collided with a bus, every inch screaming with pain. Breathing felt like a laborious task, her lungs struggling to draw in enough oxygen to stave off the encroaching haze of unconsciousness. With a determined effort, she widened her eyes, coaxing them to awaken amidst the waves of agony.

'Where the fuck am I?' she asked herself.

Noticing her surroundings, she was abruptly present. Adrenaline coursed through her veins, jolting her into full wakefulness.

The office exuded an air of timeless elegance, shrouded in an opulent darkness that seemed to defy a moment in time. Ornate, dark wood antique furniture filled the room. Tall, gothic windows allowed only a sliver of artificial light to filter through, casting a haunting glow on the books lining the shelves. The atmosphere was both regal and eerie; the walls were covered with expensive artwork–portraits of long-forgotten time before the Tri-War.

A grand, mahogany desk stood as the centrepiece, its surface cluttered with paperwork and odd keepsakes. A single, delicately carved chair awaited its occupant, its back tall and imposing.

The room seemed frozen in time, a nod to the owners' particular and peculiar taste.

The with the faint scent of leather and fresh blood lingering in the air. Arabelle searched her body for the source of bleeding. She knew the smell well from many a battlefield soaked in its scent. Except for a few superficial cuts and shallow wounds, she was remarkably free from any significant bleeding.

Arabelle paused her self-examination.

A lump of concerned filled her throat. The unmistakable scent of blood, the artificial illumination, the classic displays of wealth. This room could belong to non-other than a Hemovitalist.

"Don't worry, you aren't dying," an unknown voice startled her.

She looked up to see a clean-cut young man, a quintessential pretty boy whose appearance spoke volumes. Sharp cheekbones shaped his face, and his alabaster skin seemed to defy imperfections, smooth and flawless. The attraction of his light hazel eyes was impossible to ignore, his captivating looks in stark contrast to the tousled, dark brown hair that effortlessly fell into place, creating a charming and stylishly groomed look. She was conflicted, his demeanour exuded confidence and ease, adding to the overall charm that surrounded him. The fact that he was a Hemovitalist was obvious, yet he seemed out of place in the room, almost like a regular visitor rather than the owner of the space.

"Hi there, I'm Roland," he announced, like it was supposed to mean something to the now terrified and confused Arabelle.

Roland was impeccably dressed in well-fitted clothes that highlighted his tall and lean frame. Poised and charismatic. Arabelle didn't know whether to fight him or ask for fashion advice.

"So, here you are, at our compound, welcome. We are just waiting for the boss man. He wanted to have a word with you before you go for processing."

He had a warm smile that weirdly put Arabelle at ease, and his voice was smooth and articulate, making it easy to get lost in the conversation.

"One of our BioBots picked you up, brought you here to be … well anyway you're here now,"

"Your BioBots?" Arabelle questions.

"Yep, we have a small group that does our dirty work for us. I mean, why not? We can't always be getting our hands…"

"Covered in human blood?" Arabelle injected.

"Well, I was going to say 'Dirty' but if you want to go and get all huffy about it," Roland jokes.

Arabelle ignored his attempts at charming humour. "Processing. What do you mean before I go for processing?" she questioned.

Roland looked surprised and disappointed that he had used the term in front of a human. "Oh, nothing, just the way we describe, when you, well, donate to us." he replied cautiously.

Quillian entered the room at the perfect moment, just in time to rescue Roland from Arabelle's impending interrogation.

She recognised him immediately.

"You!" she snarled.

He smiled at the feisty beauty. "You remembered me," he mused. "I couldn't forget you—and it's amazing how if you give a BioBot a detailed enough description, it can find anyone."

Arabelle's face showed no amusement. "Do you realise how many people you have killed!"

"None," Quillian calmy replies. "If you comply, you don't get hurt. We have many, shall we say, guests who were collected by our BioBots. They arrived mostly unharmed and now live with us safe and comfortably,"

"Your BioBots destroyed my whole Kinship,"

Quillian looked genuinely confused and shocked.

"My BioBots found you about an hour's walk outside of these compound walls,"

Quillian and Arabelle shared identical expressions of confusion. Arabelle couldn't recall how she had ended up so close to the Hemo compound, while Quillian was lost in a different train of thought.

"Wait, you are from a Kinship?" He questioned. "How many people are there?"

Arabelle figured there was no point in trying to hide her Kin now. She saw the carnage as she battled the BioBots.

"Uronga, about 100 people," she replied deflated

"The Blood Bank!" Roland exclaimed loudly.

Arabelle started to wonder how much of Roland's throat she could tear out before Quillian could retaliate.

"Roland!" Quillian retorts "Show some respect,"

"But there goes our chance of surviving another decade, if the Blood... sorry Uronga is destroyed, how are we supposed to."

"Thanks Roland, you can go now," Quillian interrupted.

"I apologise for my friend," Quillian offered.

Arabelle nodded. She could see no sense in fighting.

"I never did get your name?" Quillin with a smile.

"Arabelle."

"Arabelle" Quillian repeated. His deep voice and smooth rolling tongue made her name sound like a song. She couldn't help but grin.

Quillian noticed her defences weakening and pressed on. "Listen, I'm not going to lie to you Arabelle. Yes, we do keep your kind here and yes, we do take their blood... but it's not what you think."

Arabelle eyes widen. "Oh really, not what I think... cause that's exactly what I think."

"No, it's not like we kidnap them or anything." Quillian continued. "In exchanged for food and safe shelter, we do ask, for... ongoing donations."

"And if they refuse?" Arabelle quired

"Well, most don't. It's a reciprocal agreement, one that benefits everyone."

"And if they refuse?" Arabelle repeated.

"On occasions, we have had to extract... compulsory."

Arabelle could tell he was choosing his words wisely.

"Riiight," she said sceptically "And if they want to leave?"

Quillian looked worried. "That request... would most likely, be... declined."

Arabelle's expression spoke volumes; a penetrating glare that unravelled his conscience without the need for words.

"What would you have me do? watch my people get weak, frail, die?" Quillian asked rhetorically.

Arabelle showed no emotion. She studied Quillian, attempting to detect whether his kindness and remorse was genuine or if he was trying to ensnare her as a blood slave.

Nevertheless, he was painfully handsome, appeared reasonably sincere, and currently stood as the sole obstacle between her and freedom.

She grappled with accepting the reality of the situation before her. Launching a direct assault was clearly a risky move that would likely result in her own demise. While her skills were impressive, the challenge of confronting an entire compound filled with Hemovitalists proved to be beyond her capabilities. Within her brave exterior, a conflict was brewing. A subtle, unspoken reluctance was churning in the pit of her stomach. Quillian, undeniably labelled as 'the enemy,' had introduced an unexpected element. Strangely, she had an increasing emotional connection to him growing within her heart. This realisation added an annoying layer to her internal conflict.

Arabelle scanned the room, stalling for time while attempting to strategize an escape. Roland stood quietly, observing her every move; he appeared rightly suspicious and would likely be the first to attack. Quillian, undoubtedly the alpha male, was her most worrying opponent. But he seemed enamoured with her. She had seen that look on men's faces before. She knew she could inflict maximum damage before he would snap out of his lovesick haze. But at what cost?

A brief moment of contemplation passed through Arabelle's mind, and then a gentle, sweet smile graced her lips.

"Can I use the little girls' room please?" she politely asked.

Chapter Seventeen

IN A WELL-LIT UNDERGROUND compound, Arabelle strained to hear any distant sounds that might signal danger. The cold air, tinged with a faint metallic blood smell, clung to her nostrils as she stealthily moved through narrow, winding corridors. Frustration and fear set in as there was no indication of an exit. Taking a deep breath to compose herself, she tried to think logically.

Arabelle knew that Quillian would soon realise she was missing and would likely sound the alarm. Her heart raced as she navigated the labyrinthine passages, relying solely on her instincts. The distant echoes of footsteps and muffled voices hinted at the presence of Hemovitalists. Were they searching for her, or were they simply going about their daily business?

A flicker of movement caught her eye, and she pressed herself against the wall of a doorway. A pair of guards, clad in dark uniforms, passed by, their conversation a low murmur. Arabelle's breath caught in her throat as she waited for them to move on. She couldn't afford to be discovered now.

As soon as the guards disappeared around a corner, Arabelle resumed her escape. She quickened her pace, weaving through the network of tunnels with a silent determination. Her senses heightened. She could feel the adrenaline coursing through her veins, sharpening her focus.

A distant clang echoed through the corridors, and Arabelle knew she was running out of time. The compound was vast, and she needed to find an exit before her pursuers closed in. Rounding a corner, she stumbled upon a room filled with crates and supplies. It was a storage area,

Spotting a narrow ventilation shaft in the corner of the room, Arabelle's eyes widened with a glimmer of hope. She approached it cautiously, realising that it might be her ticket to freedom. With nimble fingers, she removed the vent cover and peered into the darkness beyond.

The shaft was just wide enough for her to squeeze through. Taking a deep breath, Arabelle hoisted herself up and began crawling through the narrow passageway. The sound of her own breath and the distant hum of machinery drowned out the noise of her pursuers.

The shaft twisted and turned, leading her on a precarious journey through the bowels of the compound. Arabelle's muscles ached, and her palms grew sweaty as she navigated the cramped space. Yet the thought of freedom fuelled her determination.

Finally, after what felt like an eternity, Arabelle emerged into the cool night air. She found herself in a secluded area, surrounded by dense foliage. The moonlight filtered through the leaves, casting a silvery glow on the ground. Arabelle took a moment to catch her breath, her eyes scanning the surroundings for any signs of danger. With a new sense of purpose Arabelle sprinted as fast as her weekended legs would carry her.

After escaping the danger, when her legs could no longer carry her, she collapsed and rolled into a shallow crevice on the forest floor. Gasping for breath, she tried to inhale as much oxygen as possible. Arabelle laid there on the forest floor, trying to process the day.

She laid still, looking up at the night sky. She found herself grappling with a myriad of thoughts, a whirlwind of contemplations, but Quillian's piercing green eyes were the only thing that occupied her thoughts. The magnetic gaze of those eyes held her captive, making her feel as if she was under a spell. The warrior within her saw the enemy, and felt a sense of revenge, but the woman she was, saw the man he was, and felt a compelling attraction. She couldn't help but despise her own weakness for being unable to resist his allure.

Bursting with triumph, a familiar voice called out from above, "I've found her! I've found her!"

Chapter Eighteen

In his favourite armchair, the contours of which bore the impression of countless sittings, Dr. Stanley Cryton settled in. His weathered face etched with lines that spoke of a lifetime filled with both triumphs and regrets.

No longer at the forefront of scientific innovation, his fame now relegated to footnotes, Stanley spent most days in his favourite chair, observing the world's unfolding events through the lens of his television set. The algorithm of live-streamed content inundated him with constant updates on the lifeform he helped create—a lifeform now wreaking havoc on the world.

As his eyes valiantly resisted the pull of sleep, a familiar name jolted him awake. Squinting at the big screen, he tuned into the documentary, "Year 2076—The Year of Dr. Emily Warren."

In the glow of the broadcast, Stanley could remember a youthful Emily, her admiration for him, his instinct to mentor and nurture her talent. The laughter they once shared, the conflicts, the sense of betrayal, and, ultimately, the day when Emily shared her dreams of Nanoquarks with a team of brilliant minds. A meeting Dr Stanley Cryton was not invited to.

As the documentary unfolded, the television's flickering light painted a picture of a new world where Nanoquarks could be injected into any bloodstream, seek out and disintegrated metal structures, rendering them harmless. A technological marvel, yet, instead of awe, a sense of discomfort settled over James, the innovation felt more like a Pandora's Box than a beacon of progress.

With interest, Stanley made a subtle shift in his seat. Leaning forward, he bridged the gap between himself and the TV screen, his eyes narrowing in an effort to immerse himself fully in the unfolding scenes. The faces on the screen were familiar, there was a glint of recognition as his eyes beamed at the individual players in Emilys triumph. Dr. Oliver Anderson, the maestro of mechanical vibrations harnessed for endless energy; Dr. Maria Gonzalez, the artisan who crafted receptors with a precision that rivalled nature's lock-and-key mechanisms; Dr. Thomas Reynolds, the alchemist of enzymes, transforming metal structures into inert byproducts.

Stanley knew all the players, but he hated the game. He couldn't find pride in the achievements laid bare before him. Instead, he felt the sting of regret for the camaraderie lost, the dreams left unfulfilled, and the pain of discord that resonated within the sub-microscopic world of their treachery. A small part of him hoped the BioBots would detect and destroy any foreign object in their bloodstream, proving that he, as their creator, was invincible.

They were setting out to destroy what he had created, and he could not forgive them.

The TV screen continued with its torturous praise of the microscopic wonders—Nanoquarks—tiny warriors navigating the bloodstream, dismantling metal structures with surgical precision. Stanley shook his head, nothing more than the destroyers of his creation. He knew a better way, but no one would listen to an old man with a vested interest in BioBot survival.

James's old hands, once caressing the armrests with familiarity, now gripped them in an unspoken tension. A holographic blueprint unfolded before him, showcasing the collaborative efforts of experts in nanotechnology, materials science, biology, and robotics. He couldn't help but marvel at the intricacy of the design—the biocompatible lipid membrane, the carbon-based nanotube backbone, and miniature ion thrusters enabling navigation through the bloodstream. He felt a mixture of admiration and anger, it was a far better design than he had given credit, but his eyes, clouded with nostalgia, failed to find comfort in young Emilys achievement.

The room erupted with the applause from the vast conference room where Dr. Warren and her team had announced the success of their mission. Metalis Nanoquarks, once a dream shared among a select few, was a reality, ready to combat the BioBot threat and contribute to the end of the Tri-Species War.

The old scientist, now a spectator to a story he once co-authored, found no solace in the glow of the television. Standing, he gave into his body's yearning for rest and decided to retire for the night. Defeated by progress.

Chapter Nineteen

THE BANQUET TABLE STOOD as the centrepiece of the grand hall, a vast expanse adorned with opulence and grace. A pristine white tablecloth cascaded down its length, pooling gently on the floor. The table, extensive enough to rival a royal feast. Seafood, fresh from the depths, adorned the banquet table like a maritime masterpiece. Platters of succulent lobster tails, briny oysters on ice, and elegantly arranged homemade sushi tempted and beckoned the guests to gather and partake.

With a watchful eye, Shyla looked over at Quillian. He appeared burdened by an unseen responsibility, as he took his seat in silence at the head of the grand communal dining table.

What had once been a humble gathering to foster community spirit had evolved into a display of wealth, showcasing the lavish lifestyle embraced by the Hemovitalists.

He sighed at the arrogant banter, remembering when the discussions used to surround the defeat of the BioBots. Their destruction was once a passionate endeavour to eliminate the danger they posed, but now had gradually lost its prominence and become obscure. The BioBots weren't a major threat, but rather crafty thieves who consistently stole from the human population—the vital sustenance of the Hemovitalists.

No longer were the fervent discussions focused on shielding humanity from the BioBots' threat. The Hemovitalists had evolved, embodying a new philosophy as caretakers committed to a sustainable and eco-conscious approach to overseeing the human populace. Their perspective shifted from being protectors to becoming guardians of a fragile balance in the harvest of blood, nurturing the well-being of the human population. As a farmer would be protective of his cattle herd.

Around the table, the conversation buzzed with a palpable acknowledgment of the shifting dynamics. The Hemovitalists, previously unified in their mission, now faced the challenge of balancing necessity and morality.

Shyla felt the weight of a new era as she looked into Quillian's contemplative gaze, where the lines between predator and protector became blurred, Hemovitalists and the humans they sought to sustain locked in a symbiotic dance of life and blood.

There was a sense of tranquillity about him, as if he were deep in contemplation. Despite the fact that it was never seemed ideal, Shyla sensed that the opportune moment for a conversation with Quillian had finally arrived.

"Hey you," she offered for starters, trying to sense his mood.

"Hey," he replied.

"I have a bit of a surprise for you. I have been working on a project and I think you are going to love what I have to offer.

Quillian had grown tired of Shyla's games, her sexual innuendoes and attempts at entrapment.

"Not interested," he sighed.

Undeterred, Shyla continued, "Not interested in the location of the Blood Bank?"

And with one question, Shyla commanded Quillian's complete and undivided attention.

She grinned with pleasure at his keenness. "I have an insider, a human who has spent their entire life basically living in fear of being human. They want out and are willing to trade their entire Kin to become one of us,"

Quillan's brow furrowed in a puzzled frown. "But they can't become one of us, it's not possible to actually do that. The virus is extinct now."

"I know that, you know that ... but they don't know that." She mused. "Here's what happened. I was approached with the promise of a vaccine to help return us to 'normal.' You know, join their club, be human again or something stupid like that. And I am thinking, who the fuck wants that, right? So, in return, I kind of hinted at the fact that I could turn them into one of us, and it is amazing what people will trade for the chance to..." Shyla looked around the room, her hands gracefully gesturing to showcase her surroundings. "You know, to be one of us, join this."

Quillian found himself torn between disdain and admiration for her. While she had managed to skilfully resolved many of his problems, her methods were marked by a certain lack of scruples. He gazed at her intently, grappling with the conflicting emotions, attempting to arrive at a definitive judgment.

"Oh now, don't look at me like that. This human has told me how they live. They are the lowest of the food chain. They are a commodity; I mean, who wants to live like that? If anything, we are doing the whole kinship a favour,"

"How on Earth did you find a human mole?" Quillian asked impatiently.

"Funniest thing, they found me. Turns out their little piece of paradise isn't what it is cracked up to be."

Despite his attempts, Quillian couldn't hide his doubts, Concern crept across his face. "Don't be fooled by a human. They are way smarter than you think."

Shyla leant back, thrusting out her chest and playfully swinging her chair from side to side.

She nonchalantly shrugged, her expression a mix of disbelief and amusement.

"In just a single generation, humanity went from apex predator to the lowest tier of prey." she mused, a sardonic smile playing on her lips. "I mean, really, how intelligent can they be?"

Chapter Twenty

THE AIR, THICK WITH the fragrance of moss and damp earth, encircled Dalton as sunlight filtered through the dense foliage above. His keen eyes darted across the ground, scanning the patterns on the forest floor. He moved with a sense of purpose, nimble fingers occasionally brushing against the ferns that lined the trail. He looked like a child hunting for treasure. His shorter stature didn't hinder his youthful and charismatic presence; in fact, it may have contributed to it.

His slightly blemished and fair, sun-kissed skin on his face added to his boyish appearance. His every step was deliberate, navigating the terrain with a blend of agility and determination. The forest, a land of towering ferns and ancient trees, was a beautiful backdrop for his important search. He crouched down to inspect the imprints on the soft soil—a telltale sign of wildlife, or perhaps a clue to his quest. A sudden glint of light caught his eye. He approached a small clearing where the sunlight filtered through the leaves, revealing a clearing.

Despite Dalton's young features and shorter stature, his voice carried a commanding resonance and surprising depth. "I've found her! I've found her!" he yelled into the dense forest that surrounded the shallow crevice in the forest floor.

"Dalton?" Arabelle asked softly.

"G'Day Arabelle, fancy meeting you here." Dalton's smile was a relief. His lips curved elegantly, revealing a well-cared-for set of teeth that exemplified his unyielding optimism, even in challenging times.

Arabelle chuckled at Dalton's attempt at humour, her laughter a gentle melody in the otherwise tense atmosphere. The forest seemed to exhale a collective sigh of relief as the tension eased with Dalton's arrival.

Byron was the next to arrive, his confident stride catching everyone's attention. "Oh, thank god," he exclaimed with relief as he scrambled across the ground to reach Arabelle's side. Morrison made a less grand entrance, arriving quietly, and blending into the surroundings. Despite that, his face lit up with unmistakable relief. With hopeful eyes, Arabelle scanned the forest, eagerly awaiting the arrival of the rest of her Kin.

Dalton, sensing her optimism, offered an explanation. "This is it; we have a few injured others, but the rest are..."

"We don't know where they are," Byron interjected, attempting to spare Arabelle's feelings.

Arabelle held back her tears, her eyes reflecting the weight of the unspoken sorrow. "Madlyn?" she inquired, her voice barely above a whisper.

The silence that followed spoke the painful truth of her never seeing her best friend again. In the past, the forest teemed with activity, but now it echoed with the haunting absence of their fallen companions. The atmosphere was filled with a melancholic melody, grieving the absence of camaraderie and shared laughter.

"We think Varity was killed trying to protect her." Dalton offered, his words a sombre acknowledgment of the sacrifices made in the name of friendship and survival.

Arabelle's gaze softened as a nostalgic smile played on her lips. In the tranquil clearing, memories of Madlyn's infectious laughter and unyielding loyalty flooded Arabelle's thoughts. The absence of certain aspects in her life became more palpable in the quietude, but Madlyn's friendship emerged as a steadfast anchor, and the weight of that enduring bond that made the void more bearable.

There was a moment of silence, a pause for reflection. Arabelle and Madlyn's was the yin and yang. Their genuine camaraderie and unwavering support created a ripple effect, fostering a sense of unity and compassion in their Kinship.

The weight of death's presence hit Arabelle, and tears streamed down her face. Quickly, she wiped them away, trying to hold back the emotions that surged within her.

There was no time for mourning; she had to rally her army, gather resources, and devise a plan for payback. Revenge was an ill-conceived plan driven by emotional distress rather than strategic thinking, but she couldn't see beyond the overwhelming sense of loneliness that now consumed her.

Surrounded by what remained of her kin, Arabelle sat in solitude, a poignant symbol of sorrow.

At that precise moment, a beam of bright light shot straight up into the heavens like an illuminated pathway of Madlyn's soul travelling to a better place.

The light went unnoticed by everyone except Arabelle, who alone cast her eyes toward the sky. The unearthly glow slicing through the night sky seemed to infuse Arabelle with newfound determination, transforming grief into a fierce resolve.

Filled with a combination of astonishment and a sense of liberation, her eyes widened, her tears dried because in that precise moment, she experienced a truth that had remained concealed from all others up until that point.

A way to finally defeat the BioBots.

Chapter Twenty-One

IT WAS FINALLY TIME. Shyla leant back in her chair, savouring the sweet taste of success as she brushed her auburn hair away from her face. The intricate web of deception she had woven was finally paying off, and the satisfaction of outsmarting her human contact played across her smug smile. Her plan to exploit the gullibility of her unsuspecting accomplice had unfolded with remarkable precision.

The lure of a vaccine that promised to create superhumans had initially struck her as absurd, almost laughable. However, she recognised its potential value, not for its intended purpose, but as a means to an end. Shyla planned it as the key to gaining Quillian's favour and, more importantly, securing a steady blood supply to safeguard her clan from the looming threat of starvation. How could he not love her then?

She was tired. The journey to this pivotal moment had been laborious, requiring considerable effort on her part. The seemingly chance meeting with her human contact had been meticulously orchestrated, each step calculated to draw them closer. A subtle flirtation had set the stage for months of delicate negotiations, during which Shyla skilfully navigated the intricacies of building trust. It was a slow and patient dance, with every move calculated to breed familiarity and ensure her human counterpart felt a sense of connection.

As the relationship deepened, Shyla dangled the promise of an attainable hope—a tantalizing prospect that kept her ally invested in their collaboration. It was a masterstroke in manipulation, a delicate balance of truth and fiction that kept her human committed to the cause. Finally, when the opportune moment arrived, Shyla delivered a bold-faced lie, intertwining it with the fulfillment of the promised hope.

The gears of her elaborate scheme turned smoothly, gears lubricated with deceit and cunning. Confident in the success of her plan, Shyla revelled in the anticipation of what lay ahead. She knew the path would guide her to the blood bank, a vital source for her clan's survival. Little did Quillian know that behind the mask of cooperation and shared goals, Shyla was orchestrating a clandestine operation to ensure the prosperity of her people in the face of danger.

The door to her apartment swung open, and she stood to greet her human contact, striking a sexy yet approachable pose.

It was a familiar face that welcomed her, but not the one she was hoping for.

Roland stood, studying her pose, attempting to comprehend its meaning.

"What!?" she snapped.

"Your guest has arrived," he announced.

Shyla abandoned her pose and shot him a fierce glare. "Well, show them in!" she impatiently replied.

"Do you really think this is going to work?" he asked.

Shyla found amusement in his concern; a playful expression crossed her face. With a subtle smile, she returned to her previous pose, and with an air of confidence bordering on arrogance, she waved his concerns away, never entertaining the possibility of failure. In her mind, success was a sure thing for her plan. The human factor in this manipulative game had a mysterious drive to surpass their own limits.

To Shyla, it seemed a risky ambition, as they were willing to betray their kin for a chance at something extraordinary. She found the motivations behind this convenient alliance intriguing. Was it rooted in the deep-seated envy of their faster and stronger counterparts? Did humans feel the weight of mortality, pushing them to seek invincibility? Perhaps it was pure greed, an unquenchable thirst for power.

Or, as she suspected, was it simply a desire to be exceptional, to shine brightly above others and leave a unique legacy in history? These thoughts played in Shyla's mind like an intriguing symphony, each note revealing more about her human collaborator. Her understanding went beyond securing a blood supply; it extended to grasping the intricate web of human motivations.

Shyla found that as she delved into her unwitting ally's psyche, she marvelled at the complexity of human emotions and ambitions. It was a delicate dance of jealousy, mortality, greed, and the relentless pursuit of uniqueness. Navigating this psychological landscape was key to controlling her human counterpart and ensuring her plan's smooth execution. With each passing day, Shyla's confidence in manipulating the situation grew.

The unfolding drama between the two unlikely allies wasn't just a means to an end; it was a fascinating exploration of the human condition and how far one would go to escape normalcy.

The unsuspecting human had no idea their quest for superhuman abilities had become entangled in a grander scheme, orchestrated by the enemy to secure her clan's survival.

Roland, excused himself from the room momentarily, returning with Shyla's unsuspecting human friend.

The human looked a bit curious and nervous as they walked in. Shyla, sitting there with a kind of planned warmth, greeted them with a big smile. But under that friendly smile, she had some hidden plans.

"Welcome, welcome," Shyla chimed, her voice carrying a melodic charm that belied the complexity of the situation. "Please do come in, have a seat." Her invitation held an almost theatrical quality, as if the stage had been set for a secret performance where each participant played a role, unaware of the tragic script.

The human accomplice hesitated before taking a seat, Shyla's eyes sparkled with a mixture of friendliness and shrewdness. She smiled, a seemingly warm smile that was betrayed by a subtle edge—a masterful blend of charm and manipulation. It was a smile that promised collaboration yet hinted at the complexities that lay beneath the surface.

The human, caught in the crossfire of politeness and suspicion, navigated the room with a sense of uncertainty, oblivious to the machinations weaving around them. The furniture, carefully arranged, to give Shyla an unconscious strategic edge. Each chair, every ornament, held silent echoes of the tactical positioning that mirrored the invisible chessboard where alliances and betrayals were being plotted.

Shyla signalled to a chair. "Please sit, sit."

Roland, the orchestrator of this meeting, positioned himself in the background, silently observing the unfolding drama. Hi presence was to serve as an unspoken recognition of the collaboration between superhuman hunter and her human prey, a partnership that teetered on the edge of necessity and manipulation.

Seated now, the human accomplice couldn't shake the feeling that they were stepping into a world where the ordinary rules no longer applied. Shyla's continuous smile, though friendly, suggested she knew more than she let on, carrying with it a hidden plan. The atmosphere in the room was filled with unexpressed emotions, creating a palpable energy that underscored the gravity of the partnership, cleverly concealed beneath the guise of common interests.

The human took a deep breath. "You know why I am here, then." They asked firmly, trying to hide the fear in their voice.

Shyla tilted her head, conveying a message of reassurance, as if to said, 'There's no need to be afraid.' "of course, I do. I have been looking forward to meeting you," she replied.

As the talk went on, directed by Shyla's well-picked words, the room turned into a stage for a deceitful show. Every gesture, every glance, carried a hidden meaning—a mysterious dance where alliances were formed not only with words but also with the unspoken language of concealed intentions and hidden plans.

The human relaxed. Feeling safe and assured in such a luxurious and hospitable setting. Oblivious to the plan unravelling beneath them, ignorant that their ignorance would not only destroy their kinship but give Shyla's clan unprecedented power.

The stage was set, actors in position, each playing their part in a story that's ending had already been written.

Chapter Twenty-Two

ON A BEAM, IN THE HEART of a bustling factory, an inconspicuous stainless-steel bolt, camouflaged among its countless counterparts, found itself on the verge of rewriting history. A subtle breach in the feeding tube started a nearly imperceptible drip every three minutes, landing with precision on the unassuming bolt. Over the course of three years, one week, and four days, this relentless drip caused the bolt to rust gradually, weakening its grip under the relentless pressure.

A faint vibration set the bolt in motion, and it descended onto the conveyor belt, seamlessly blending into the ongoing journey. Progressing into a high-pressure chamber, the rogue bolt became a discreet saboteur in the dance of the factory's internal mechanisms. Exiting the chamber, it glided noiselessly across the sterile floor, generating a spark of static electricity unnoticed by the facility's automated intelligence.

In a twist of fate, this minuscule spark found a highly flammable substance that had subtly leaked onto the conveyor belt. In an instant, the air ignited, triggering fiery explosions within the enclosed chamber. The bolt, propelled like a bullet, punctured the ceiling, creating a substantial breach. This breach allowed a potent beam of light to pierce the night sky, casting a signal visible for kilometres in all directions.

For two brief minutes, the radiant beam gestured like a tractor beam, providing a guiding light to the BioBot facility. Little did the automated intelligence realise that an inconspicuous bolt, weathered by time and pressure, had orchestrated a silent rebellion, leaving a luminous mark on the secret operations hidden within the factory's walls.

DALTON FELT A PAIN in his chest as he watched Arabelle sitting alone, surrounded by what was left of her kin. She was such a lonely figure of grief. He couldn't grasp the reason behind why fate, the universe, God, or whatever one believed in, had dealt such a harsh blow to a woman who had devoted her life to safeguarding others.

Dalton watched Arabelle's beautiful face as it transformed from despair to optimism. He pondered over the mysterious chain of thoughts that could instigate such a rapid shift in her mood.

"Look," Arabelle uttered calmly, her gaze fixed upon the night sky. Dalton, his head slightly cocked, inquired, "At what?"

Arabelle's arm rose to point at a beam of light, but by the time she directed Dalton's attention, it had vanished. Dalton's head swivelled around like a dog tracking a swift moving ball. Arabelle couldn't help but smile at his endearing confusion.

She let out a disappointed sigh as she exclaimed, "Dam it, it's gone."

Dalton was curious now. "What was it?"

"An exceptionally brilliant and precisely collimated light beam of considerable intensity, to the extent that its visibility extends throughout the lower atmospheric layers," Arabelle replied playfully.

Dalton gave Arabelle a searching gaze. "What?" he asked impatiently.

"What kind of energy source could produce a light so intense it refracts into the sky?" she mused.

Dalton, still without a clue of what she was talking about, looked at Bryon for guidance.

"A BioBot's energonixium," Byron replies. "But a single BioBot lacks the power to generate such brilliance,"

"Correct, but how do the BioBots sustain their factory operations?" Arabelle inquired, anticipation gleaming in her raised eyebrows as she prepared to unveil her plan.

Byron's smile widened with the same realisation. "They sacrifice redundant models and harness their collective power through banks of energonixium," he answered.

Arabelle seized Byron's face, her touch sending a flutter through him. "Exactly," she whispered, her proximity causing his heart to race.

"What the fuck are you two talking about?" Dalton, slightly jealous and still confused, retorted.

"I don't know how, and I don't care why, but we have just been shown the precise location of a BioBot factory," Arabelle replied with a wink.

Chapter Twenty-Three

PERCHED ATOP A DILAPIDATED five story building, Arabelle and Byron took in the deserted cityscape from their elevated vantage point. The rooftop, worn and weathered, creaked softly beneath their weight as they surveyed the surroundings. Their position offered a panoramic view of the desolation surrounding them. Broken windows and crumbling facades whispered tales of a once vibrant city now lost to the war. The footpaths are covered in elongated shadows caused by the flickering solar streetlights.

"That's definitely it," Arabelle whispered, gesturing at the building below.

"It doesn't look like much," replied Bryon, still uncertain that Arabelle had found the right place.

"Trust me, from the angle of that light I saw, the approximate distance and an unobscured projection rate. Its point of emission was somewhere around here. I have discounted half the buildings in this block due to size and structure integrity. This one is it. I feel it,"

The sun gradually ascended, its warm rays casting a soft, golden glow over the awakening city. As she took a deep breath, Arabelle embraced the coolness of the morning air, a refreshing reminder of the day's potential. Her expression blossomed into a smile, a silent acknowledgment of the beauty that unfolded with the dawn. However, her daydream was abruptly interrupted by the crunching sounds of a massive garage door opening nearby.

Reacting swiftly, Arabelle instinctively lowered herself, finding a strategic position that offered both concealment and a vantage point. Her keen eyes remained just above the edge, giving her the ability to witness the unfolding events below.

"Told you," She whispered to Byron.

As the garage door fully ascended, a procession of BioBots emerged. Arabelle observed silently as group after group of the Biomechanical entities streamed out, purposefully dispersing into the city for their daily task of human harvesting.

THE CITYSCAPE UNDERWENT a subtle metamorphosis over the course of twelve long hours, as the sun descended towards the horizon, painting the sky in hues of orange and pink. The beauty of the sunset lost to a tired and sunburnt Arabelle, and her equally tanned and bored companion. The BioBots, having completed their assigned duties, began their return journey to the enigmatic factory.

"Now we know they leave their factory relatively unguarded for twelve hours of the day," Byron noted, a sly grin playing on his lips as he exchanged a knowing glance with Arabelle.

The duo, concealed in the shadows, now possessed valuable information that would shape their next move.

The next day, in the scorching mid-morning sun, the unyielding heat pounded the city as Arabelle, Byron, Dalton, and Morrison cautiously made their way through the deserted alleyways. Shattered glass shimmered in the sunlight, reflecting the harsh rays onto the worn footpaths below. The towering skeletons of buildings, once proud monuments, now stood as silent witnesses to the passage of time. As the small group of humans pressed forward on their quest, the unforgiving sunlight belted down on their skin.

The city, stripped of its nocturnal mystique, unfolded in the harsh brilliance of the day. Vines, resilient and opportunistic, clung to the sides of structures, their green tendrils a vibrant contrast against the muted tones of decay. The relentless heat filled the air with a tangible stillness, broken only by the occasional groans of metal structures swaying in the warm breeze. Overhead, rusted signs dangled; their messages indecipherable in the harsh sunlight, remnants of a once vibrant commerce that had long faded away.

The BioBot factory, a metallic behemoth on the outskirts, stood imposingly against the azure sky. The heatwaves distorted the air around the towering structures, casting mirages that shimmered in the distance. Arabelle's sense of empowerment persisted, transformed by the stark light of day. The factory's shadows, elongated in the intense sunlight, whispered of secrets waiting to be uncovered amid the city's midday silence.

With a determined look in her eyes, Arabelle guided the group towards the grand entrance. The closer they got, the more noticeable the tension in the air became, almost suffocating in its intensity. Arabelle turned to the team, her voice low but firm.

"We've got one shot at this. Dalton, cover our backs. Byron, keep an eye on the control panels. Morrison..."

Morrison's anxiety was palpable, and Arabelle sighed inwardly. She put a reassuring hand on his shoulder. "Stick close, Morrison. We've got this."

The entrance creaked open, revealing the eerie glow of the factory's interior. Navigating the corridors with the precision of a disorganised collection of cats, the group ventured inside.

The periodic pulse of the machinery surrounded them, like a heartbeat echoing through the cold metal walls.

Arabelle, always the leader, guided them deeper into the heart of the factory. Nervous hope surged in their hearts like static energy as they made their way towards the central control room, obvious in its location due to the myriad of exposed electrical wires elegantly converging in its direction. These conspicuous channels formed a visual network, subtly guiding their way like metallic arteries towards a central electrical meeting point. The distant clanging of metal and the occasional hiss of steam created an unsettling magnum opus that mirrored the group's escalating nerves.

Ahead, two BioBot guards stood sentinel, occasionally walking in different directions as per their protection protocols. The group halted, Arabelle motioning for everyone to crouch low against the walls. They observed the patrol pattern of the BioBots, waiting for the opportune moment to make their move. With synchronised precision far beyond their skill set, the group timed their advance, creeping forward as the BioBots turned away.

They hugged the shadows, using crates and machinery for cover, inching closer to their objective with every careful step. As they neared closer Dalton could feel every heartbeat echoing in his ears. Scared beyond belief. With a silent signal from Byron, he darted across the open space, heart pounding as he prayed to evade detection. Whether through sheer luck or calculated skill, they managed to slip past undetected.

In the control room, Arabelle approached the console, her fingers dancing over the keys. She found herself facing the array of buttons, their functions a mystery to her. Uncertain of where to begin, the idea of simply switching everything off seemed like a sensible starting point.

The hum of the machines began to subside, replaced by an eerie silence. The factory, once a non-stop store of activity, now stood still.

Arabelle sensed it was too easy. She felt that something was amiss, but the machines had stopped, and there was no point in worrying the others.

"We did it," Arabelle declared, her eyes reflecting a mixture of triumph and fear. "Now, let's make our way back. Stay sharp, everyone."

As they retraced their steps, the tension lingered. Shadows seemed to move in the corners of the dimly lit corridors, and every distant sound sent shivers down Morrison's spine. Roland kept a vigilant watch, his eyes scanning for any signs of danger, waiting for the moment he could spring into action and impress Byron.

Morrison, however, struggled to shake off his anxiety. Each step felt like a heavy burden, and the ominous atmosphere of the factory seemed to intensify. Arabelle noticed his unease and, with a nod to the others, fell back to walk beside him.

"We're almost there, Morrison. You've got this," she whispered, her words a reassurance against the lingering uncertainty.

For no reason other than instinct, Arabelle stopped. It was just too easy.

Byron sensed her conflicted thoughts.

"We should burn this place to the ground," he suggested. "This was too easy. We've missed something, we need to go next level."

"You're right," Arabelle replied. "About the easy part, but not about destroying the place. They would have expected that. Which means they would have wanted us to do it. Why?"

"Who cares, why? One less factory is one less generation of BioBot's being made," Byron replied.

As Arabelle contemplated the situation, her thoughts raced. "Stopping production and destroying the place seems too straightforward," she mused. There was an inkling in her mind, a suspicion that the BioBots were concealing something more sinister, perhaps hiding humans within their confines. This wasn't merely a manufacturing plant; it felt like a storage facility for humans, or maybe even a processing plant for blood harvest. A nagging feeling urged her to delve deeper into the mysteries that lurked within.

The realisation hit her. The BioBots wanted them to shut it all down, burn it to the ground, and retreat. It was a trap laid out in plain sight. Therefore, she concluded, they needed to defy the apparent simplicity of destruction and take the opposite route. Investigate further, don't play into the hands of the BioBots; She needed to unveil the truth.

Arabelle looked down the long corridor. Door after identical door lined the hallway. Each individual door was shut and securely locked with its own padlock.

A long row of identical padlocks. Every single one was tightly closed.

Arabelles eyes fixed on a single padlock. Identical to the others, with a slight difference. It was welded shut, defying any key to open it. The door was never to be opened.

"That one! there!" she exclaimed. Rushing to the door halfway down the corridor.

She forcefully struck the robust handle of her Katana against the secured padlock. Initially unyielding, it stubbornly held its ground. Undeterred, she struck it again, noticing a subtle, hairline crack began to emerge at the weakest point of the weld. Another forceful blow, and the lock started to loosen. With a determined yell, she summoned all her strength and delivered a final, powerful strike. The padlock, unable to withstand her might any longer, surrendered, clattering to the floor in submission.

A sudden rush of fear surged through her body as she realised the lock may have been, not to stop her from getting in, but to stop whatever was locked in there from getting out.

Her companions, realising the same thing, braced themselves—scared but determined. They then turned their attention to Arabelle, seeking guidance.

"Get ready for anything" she commanded and unleashed a powerful kick, breaking the door wide open.

In a moment of uncertainty, Arabelle burst into the room, her presence immediately capturing the attention of thirty-six pale and frightened faces. Each one wore the marks of confinement, some showing signs of enduring weeks of captivity, while others seemed wearied by only a few days.

Arabelle's eyes roamed over the expressions, and amidst the sea of unfamiliar faces, she locked eyes with just one.

"I thought you were dead!" she exclaimed; her eyes fixated on the familiar face.

Tear-filled eyes met Arabelle's stare, and she couldn't escape the depth of despair reflected in them. An unmistakable anguish etched across that familiar face served as a confirmation of Arabelles worst fears.

"Without her, I am dead." Verity replied.

Chapter Twenty-Four

SURVEYING HER SURROUNDINGS, Arabelle took in her new Kinships home. The rainforest cave was a remnant of the first Kin who had hidden out in the forest during the third war. Inside, a grand chamber with damp, cool air allowed the walls to bloom with a soft, pretty fungus. Wooden platforms along the walls served as living spaces, separated by hanging vines. A gentle stream meandered through, harmonizing with the sounds of the rainforest. Ingenious adaptations, like natural shelves and hammocks, made it a comfortable dwelling. Openings in the cave provided ventilation and light. It did not have the charm of Uronga, but it felt safe.

Arabelle's new kinship numbered less than forty, but she felt better about having the people around her. Her 'less people, less problems' motto seemed stupid in the wake of Madlyn's death. She valued each and every life and the support they gave. The cave would have comfortably housed a much smaller group, but no one complained about the cramped conditions.

"Tell me what happened, how did Madlyn die." Arabelle struggled to speak the words clearly.

Varity fought back tears. "The Hemoes took her."

Arabelle was shocked into attention. "What? the Hemoes were at the attack?"

"No, I mean, I don't know, but I saw her leaving with two Hemoes. I tried to get to her, to stop them, but with everything going on..." Verity sighed, a deep regretful sigh.

Arabele needed answers "so, she could still be alive then, everyone tell me exactly what happened, what did you see?"

Voices clamoured around Arabelle, a mixture of eager voices fighting for attention. Each person attempting to share their version of events, recount their lived experiences, and present their theories on who was responsible for the massacre. The cave filled with a mix of emotions, ranging from urgency to frustration, as everyone tried to speak to Arabelle. Her pulse quickened, a torrent of thoughts racing through her mind as she grappled with the conflicting statements laid out before her. Witness after witness painted a fragmented account, leaving her mind a tangled mess of confusion.

She turned to Verity, nodding in a gesture that concealed the storm of emotions beneath the surface. Supposedly, sympathy should have been offered, but a mask of blame covered Arabelle face. She found herself holding Verity accountable for Madlyn's death, a silent accusation lingering in her eyes.

Arabelle's mind wrestled with unspoken thoughts. She should have reached out to console Verity, to bridge the gap between them, but an underlying resentment festered. Despite the professed love that echoed between them, Arabelle couldn't help but measure it against the deep, platonic bond she shared with Madlyn.

Arabelle sat amidst her Kin, attempting to appear unfazed, concealing the turmoil within her. She strived not to show the fear or concern for Madlyn, all while wrestling with the effort to make sense of the world around her. Varity burst into laughter at something someone had said and Arabelle felt her anger surge. To enjoy a moment in a moment like this!

Feeling compelled to take action, Arabelle couldn't bear sitting still any longer. Guided by the ache in her heart and Varity's words, she knew she had to develop a plan. However, surrounded by people, she found it challenging to focus. She needed solitude to think clearly and distance herself emotionally. Arabelle understood herself well, recognizing that, in moments like these, the presence of others offered little comfort.

Arabelle's muscles tensed as she stood, the weight of determination settling in her bones. The damp air of the cave was left behind as she stepped into the surrounding bush.

"Where are you going?" Verity stood at the cave entrance.

"I... just can't stay here," Arabelle offered, her gaze fixed on the uncertain path ahead. "I've got to go."

Chapter Twenty-Five

ARABELLE'S PLAN WAS straightforward: locate a Hemo, tail them to their compound, and negotiate the release of Madlyn. However, as the third hour of her perch in the tree approached, doubt crept into her mind about the soundness of her strategy. As she exerted pressure on her leather boot, she felt a sudden cramp in her foot while using it to stabilize herself against the crevice in the tree trunk. Gripping the bark tightly, she could feel the rough texture wearing into her hand. Her muscular thighs pressed firmly against the solid branch, providing a sense of security to her athletic frame.

Hungry, Arabelle found herself stealthily trailing a large Kiwi bird, unwittingly leading her into the path of a group of Hemovitalists. They were lost and engrossed in a heated argument over directions, had provided the perfect distraction for Arabelle. Seizing the opportunity, she hastily sprayed a concoction of pee-wee mix over her clothes and hid.

The blend of dog and human urine was intended to mask the human scent, an age-old trick whose effectiveness remained uncertain. Nevertheless, the stroke of good fortune that allowed her to go unnoticed before they could catch a whiff of her scent proved to be a life-saving twist of luck.

From her vantage point, several metres above the ground, Arabelle could see the group and their interactions. The haphazard way they decided which direction to go in and the human way they interacted. For a brief moment she forgot they were the enemy.

"The sun's going down soon, I vote we find shelter," a short stocky Hemovitalist announced.

"Well, I vote that we all know that." a younger male replied sarcastically.

"Well, I vote that you're an idiot for leading us on this goose chase," an angry, tired male interrupted.

The younger male puffed out his chest "well I vote..."

"I vote we stop voting!" An older woman exclaimed.

ARABELLE SMILED AT the unintentionally comical banter, the group was obviously not organised nor on the hunt for human blood. She relaxed despite not knowing the reason for them being so far from the known Hemo Colonies in the city. Arabelle felt a little safer and felt sorry for them. She frowned immediately, angry at herself for seeing the softer side of her sworn enemy.

Arabelle corrected her mindset and contemplated an attack. She was outnumbered, but it wasn't the first time she had fought against the odds. Arabelle assessed the group for weakness. The fat one would be slow, the older one would be weaker, the young one looked inexperienced, maybe if he panicked it would give her the edge she needed.

Movement in the undergrowth stopped her mental attack, and she looked in the direction of the noise. Her heart started to race as she tuned into the sound of footsteps from the undergrowth. She looked over at the Hemovitalist, they either didn't know or didn't care what was coming, still totally consumed with which way they should proceed.

"Well, I vote that one of us needs to be voted in as leader."

Arabelle's foot tingled as pins and needles started to overcome her squashed foot. She dared not move, not now. The unknown third party was close now and the Hemovitalist lack of concern was worrying. They were not threatened which meant they didn't fear what was coming or even worse, they knew what was coming.

Arabelle's throat was dry, she tried to swallow but the lack of saliva tickled her throat and the urge to cough started to build in her oesophagus. She pressed her lips hard together and shook her head as if to will the feeling to go away. Any outburst now would be disastrous.

"What is that?" a voice from the Hemo group asked.

The whole group was now staring in the direction of the uninvited guest who was about to appear through the vegetation.

Arabelle's eyes darted between the Hemoes and the moving undergrowth. She held her breath.

A long slender, curved black beak parted the leaves, followed by a rounded body covered with shaggy brown feathers. Arabelle let out a shallow controlled breath and rolled her eyes at the irony.

"It's just a Kiwi!" one of the Hemovitalist declared.

The solid bird jumped, turned, and retreated all in one motion. The Hemovitalist were not a predator, but it was unable to tell the difference between them and its primary killer, the humans.

Arabelle wiggled her toes and shifted her weight as the Hemovitalist discussion continued. The sympathetic feeling from earlier had disappeared and was now replaced with an angry impatience as the Hemoes decided to make camp under her hiding place.

Vulnerable until dawn Arabelle had no choice but to stay in her awkward position. A plan had developed in her head, uncomfortable and cold she waited for sunrise.

ARABELLE AWOKE WITH a sudden jolt, and her immediate instinct was to look down at the Hemoes. They were nowhere to be found.

"Fuck!" she muttered. A simple 'sleep-in, of all things have thwarted her intention to follow them.

She stretched her legs out, wincing at the pain of her uncomfortable slumber.

"Are you coming or not?" a voice from afar inquired kindly. Arabelle turned towards the source of the question. The younger male Hemo stood there, waiting.

Arabelle instinct was to grip her sword. "You don't need that, we would have killed you when your snoring gave away your position," he stated calmy.

"I don't snore," Arabelle retorts.

"Yeah, actually you do, but don't worry I won't tell Quillian," he cheekily replied.

Arabelle's eyebrows shot up, her eyes widening in surprise. The young man's casual familiarity and his presumptuous remarks about Quillian left her visibly taken aback.

"Like I would even care" Arabelle replied as she started climbing down the tree.

"Yeah, actually you do, but don't worry I won't tell Quillian," he repeated.

Arabelle shot him a glance that clearly conveyed, 'Oh great, we have a comedian.' The corners of her lips tightened into a subtle snare, and her eyes, briefly rolling, hinted at a mix of exasperation and scepticism. The young man, unperturbed, met her stare with an easy-going smile, as if revelling in his perceived wit.

"Where's the rest of you?" Arabelle asked as she approached the young Hemo.

"They couldn't take your snoring anymore and left." He quipped as he walked away, gesturing her to follow.

She studied the way he held himself, head held high with a self-assured stance that seemed out of place for someone so young. In her mind, she envisioned the clash of blades, easily predicting how she would dominate him in a fight. Yet, he met her look with a calm demeanour, a lack of fear that should have been present in the face of an impending defeat.

His friendly banter and charm were clear in the way he engaged with others, but Arabelle couldn't shake the feeling of distrust that lingered within her. It wasn't just a matter of disliking him; it was a gut instinct, a subtle warning that hinted he was either too naïve to understand the harsh realities or too cocky to acknowledge them.

Survival in their unforgiving world required more than just confidence and a friendly facade, and Arabelle couldn't afford to trust him just yet.

She would follow him, endure his foolish stories, and, should he make a misstep, she wouldn't hesitate to end him in an instant.

THE OFFICE CRIED OUT for a good cleaning, falling short of his meticulous standards, especially with an impending guest. Nevertheless, Quillian tried desperately to exude an air of casual composure. The news that Arabelle had returned to the compound of her own accord thrilled him. As he awaited her, he shifted in his seat, experimenting with various nonchalant poses to project an appearance of unruffled indifference. The strategic manoeuvring seemed to be effective, successfully concealing the underlying excitement. However, before he could settle into a position that truly captured a confident nonchalance, Arabelle entered the room, startling him into his true self.

"Oh, you're here, welcome, come in, sit, down, or stand, whatever you're comfortable with." he smiled.

Arabelle smiled back. She couldn't help being charmed by his nerves.

"So, it must have been a classified operation, right? Code brown, everyone! Operation Porcelain Infiltration!" Quillian stated with a wink.

"What?" Arabelle replied, somewhat bemused.

"Use the bathroom... days ago... remember, you said ... little girl's room, must have been a number two, joke... anyway, to what do I owe the pleasure," he asked nervously.

Arabelle stood with an air of stern authority near the couch, giving the impression that she might casually take a seat and unwind. Yet, her posture remained resolute, subtly teasing the idea of relaxation without ever relinquishing her firm stance.

"Madlyn," she finally spoke "two of your goons took her."

Quillian laughed. "Firstly, I don't have 'goons' but thanks for asking and secondly, I don't know who Madlyn is."

Arabelle's face was unconvinced.

Quillian continued "we haven't accepted any new guest for weeks now. Honestly if she were here, I would tell you."

"Why should I trust you?"

"Have I ever giving you any reason not to?" Quillian asked. "So, who is Madlyn?"

Arabelle's heart felt like a heavy rock, dragging her down with sorrow. Tears pricked at her eyes as she spoke. "She is my best friend. My only friend really. I thought she was dead but recently I was given some information that might give me hope she is still alive." She swallowed hard. "Taken by the Hemoes... vitalists" she corrected herself. "If you don't have here, then she probably is dead." Arabelle's eyes searched Quillian's handsome face for answers, he felt her pain and it rendered him defenseless.

"I'm so sorry. If that is the case, then your friend is gone. I promise you, she is not here."

Arabelle slumped as the emotion weight physically crushed her.

Quillian looked genuinely remorseful. His words came softly
"So let the tears be a gentle rain,
Nourishing the soil where love remains.
In the garden of remembrance, we sow,
Seeds of joy, from which memories grow.

With every sunset, a sunrise anew,

In the moments of time, love shines through.

Death, the bridge to an eternal song,

A journey of the soul, forever strong."

Arabelles face was a mixture of astonishment and affection. "That's beautiful" she replied.

Quillian nodded. "It makes me feel like, love is ceaseless. Even as their mortal voices fade, the resonance of their life can still be heard, I find that comforting,"

Arabelle's heart felt lighter, like a balloon set free. The heavy sadness that had clung to her seemed to drift away, leaving a warm feeling inside. With a deep breath, she let go of the grief that had been holding her captive. It was still there, lingering in the background like a distant memory, but it no longer had power over her.

With Quillian's beautiful words and the simple belief that love would never die, she felt the tightness in her jaw relaxed, and all the knots in her stomach were finally coming undone. A warm feeling started to grow inside her, like a cozy blanket wrapping around her heart. It was like a friendly whisper telling her that things were going to be okay.

"Can I get you a drink?" Quillian inquired.

"Sure" Arabelle replied, looking around the room. Every detail exuded sophistication and refined taste. The room had tasteful and well-chosen furnishings, featuring a rich mahogany desk that commanded attention. The leather chair behind the desk spoke of comfort and elegance, inviting anyone seated to indulge in luxury. An organised bookshelf displayed a curated collection of leather-bound volumes, reflecting both knowledge and aesthetic discernment. It was a glimpse into the world of the man who never failed to make her heart flutter with every lingering glance.

"Nice office," she said genuinely.

Her interest excited Quillian. "Really, you like it?" he replied. "I kept all my favourite things here."

He moved alongside her, explaining the array of various trinkets, and unravelling their intriguing tales. Despite his captivating narratives, Arabelle was oblivious to his words. Her attention fixated solely on his full lips as they moved seductively, shaping the words he shared.

He reached out and brushed his fingers against her arm. A subtle energy surged through her. It was the first time their skin had made contact, and in ignited her.

Jolted by the visceral response to his touch, she stared into his eyes. His eyes reflected the same astonishment mirrored in hers. An ordinary encounter turning into a charged exchange of shared astonishment and the promise of something magnetic and extraordinary.

Arabelle poised herself, anticipating the moment Quillian would take the lead—whether with a kiss, another tender touch, a whisper in her ear. Suspended in anticipation, she scarcely breathed, her senses heightened in her silent expectancy.

Abruptly and unexpectedly, Quillian grabbed her shoulders and shoved her away.

Chapter Twenty-Six

ARABELLE FELL HARD onto the couch. She gasped on impact as she sunk deeply into the soft leather.

"Are you okay" a concerned Quillan asked.

She looked at him for a moment before answering. Amused and intrigued by the notion that a suppositively blood thirsty Hemovitalist would show such regard.

She smiled sweetly "I'm fine." she replied.

"Yes, you are." Quillan beamed as he climbed over her legs and positioned himself directly above her.

Arabelle looked into his eyes. The pale blue of his iris complemented the dark grey pupil it surrounded. From this distance his eyes lost the stark washed out look of a Hemo, up close they were alluring, like a pale ocean of desire.

"What?" he self-consciously asked, "Do my eyes freak you out?"

"No," she breathed. "Quite the contrary,"

Quillian's muscular hand skimmed lightly over her jawline and down her exposed neck, his fingertips tickling her skin lightly.

Arabelle's longing eyes still connected with his, her tongue running over her bottom lip. She squeezed her lips tightly together, slightly clenching her jaw. "I never did get that drink," she mumbled.

Quillian's tender, caressing lips found their way to the sensitive skin of her neck and her words faded into soft moans. Giving in to the tingling sensations darting through her body, she tilted her head to give him greater access.

The devastation of the outside world, the expectation of hate, and the anguish of loss all melted away from her being. The guilt of experiencing pleasure replaced by a desire to feel anything other than that guilt. It had been forever since she last felt pleasure on this level and her desperate hands slid down Quillian's hard torso, rubbing over the swelling growing beneath his dark trousers. The outline of it was huge compared to her small hands. She trembled as her hands frantically reached for his zipper, craving him deep inside her.

Moving his muscular arms around her waist and pushing her body further into the soft leather, Quillian laid over her. He clutched her face lovingly and pressed his lips hard onto hers, his tongue commanding her mouth and pleasuring his own.

There was no turning back. Stretching the low neckline of her top, Quillian impatiently tore the material in half, all the way down to her navel. His aggression shocked Arabelle, but the slightest of fear turned to desire when he clasped her full breasts, pulling them to rest over the worn cup of her bra. She hesitated, feeling self-conscious about her practical and unsexy underwear.

Quillian was undeterred, his tongue twirled around her hard nipples. He whipped the shirt from his broad shoulders and dropped it onto the carpet. Her embarrassment was destroyed by beautiful chest adorned with a natural, untamed layer of hair.

Arabelle began unbuckling his leather belt. The heaviness slid through her hands with ease as she inclined her body; her face inching close to his swelling outline. Pulling his pants down in one swift, hungry movement, revealing his imposing member only centimetres from her beautiful blue eyes. She watched it bounce momentarily in front of her. Arabelle glanced up. Quillian's apologetic face made her laugh. He looked worried.

"You scared?" she whispered.

"Are you?" he replied.

Arabelle let out a deep sigh. "Terrified," she smirked.

Quillian lost the moment with sudden concern, but his worry turned to a pleasured groan as Arabelle took him deep into her mouth. He shut his eyes and gently entwined his fingers with her hair. His hips smoothly swinging back and forth.

Although Arabelle was not experienced with such matters, instinct took over and she expertly devoured him. Quillian felt selfish in his pleasure. He wanted more of her.

"Lay back," he demanded, as his hands gripped her jeans and tugged them down to her ankles with surprising speed.

Arabelle could feel herself wet and raging, readying with anticipation.

Resting her thighs on his shoulders, Quillian propped himself on his elbows and drove his mouth and tongue into her. She could feel a blissful build up growing inside of her as his speed increased, and he introduced his fingers. The overwhelming pleasure growing inside of her forced her legs to shake with a powerful release.

"I want you," she gasped, a light glow covering her face.

"You got me," Quillian responded.

Throwing the last of her clothes from her beautiful body, Arabelle climbed onto Quillian. Her sexual appetite was at fever pitch, and she violently rode the Hemovitalist without fear or remorse. Quillian let out a guttural growl of excitement. He could no longer contain himself. Throwing Arabelle onto her back, he spread her legs wide and aligned himself.

Her eyes locked with his. "Yes," she hissed.

Quillian pushed deep inside her. Forcing himself in, retracting slowly and then slamming it hard back into her body, his hips touching hers. He began viciously fucking her. The primal instincts had taken over both their desperate bodies in need of a hard, fast connection, deriving only pleasure from one another.

Burying her head into his shoulder, she bit down hard on the skin, taking the painful pleasure. Her nails dragged down his back with an animalistic excitement, the areas being touched with her short claws now reddening. The stronger he fucked, the louder she screamed, waves and waves of pleasure consuming her body.

Quillian paced slowed, as he became aware of his strength and his growing lack of control. He had forgotten how fragile humans could be.

"You okay?" he asked quietly.

Arabelle's face filled with disappointment. "Don't fucking stop!" she protested.

Quillian complied. Leaning into her ear and sensually sucking on the lobe, he whispered, "Turn over." Biting her bottom lip hard, Arabelle moaned a little as he left her body. She rolled onto her stomach and up onto her knees, arching her back, presenting herself to him.

Grasping her hips, he sank himself into her with ease. The thrust of his hips crashed faster and faster into her. Arabelle let out a primal scream. She could feel a shot of electric pleasure shoot up her spine. She dug her face into the pillow and cried in sheer bliss, her legs quaking on the verge of release.

Quillian shut his eyes and leant his head back. The sensation grew stronger than he had ever felt before. He grabbed Arabella around the waist and lifted her off the couch. Slamming her whole body into his. She shrieked with a mighty climax as he simultaneously expelled inside her. The two entwined bodies collapsing onto the couch.

Quillian clasped Arabelle's chin, and turned her head for their lips to meet again, panting from exhaustion and desire. Her tongue eagerly explored his mouth, flawlessly moving with his.

In that moment, she knew she craved everything about him. He was a blissful indulgence to which she was instantly addicted.

Quillian rested his forehead on Arabelle's cheek and wrapped his arms around her naked body. She enraptured him.

They closed their eyes, shutting out the world and surrendering to darkness. In that moment, time seemed to pause, and they were able to exchange a shared breath connected in the stillness.

"Are you scared?" Arabelle asked.

"Terrified," Quillian replied.

Chapter Twenty-Seven

SHYLA CONFIDENTLY ENTERED the office, anticipating to find Quillian alone. To her surprise, she discovered Arabelle, naked and satisfied, perched on the side of the desk, still sweating from their recent encounter.

The office was a chaotic scene, with papers strewn about and furniture pushed aside, bearing witness to their enthusiastic activity. The destruction amused Arabelle as she sat waiting for her lover to return. Her body ached with pleasure and pain, and she loved not being able to discern which was which.

Shyla, a woman of striking beauty, possessed all the qualities one could desire. However, upon encountering Arabelle in her complete splendour, she found herself intimidated by the sheer perfection before her.

"Well, if it isn't the infamous Arabelle," she stated boredly.

Arabelle scrambled to get her clothes but calmly responded, "Correct, and you are?"

"Wondering where Quillian is?" Shyla replied coldly.

Arabelle shrugged, like his whereabouts were of no concern to her, further insulting and infuriating Shyla. "Don't know, I'm not his keeper." She said as she dressed.

"Enjoy your moment blood-bag." Shyla retorted.

Arabelle smirked at her pretty red-haired adversary. "I did enjoy it," she replied.

Shyla studied Arabelle. "Hmm, you are as feisty as your reputation aren't you. The human warrior Queen who leads and protects, all the while complaining about her role as the hero,"

Arabelle felt a chill creeping up her spine as the woman effortlessly seemed to reveal an unsettling depth of knowledge about her. Despite this, Arabelle maintained her composure, showing no outward hint of worry, firmly holding her ground.

"If you know my reputation then you would know not to mess with me," She replied.

Shyla took a step closer, her face now within an inch of Arabelles. "But you don't know me darling, what's my reputation?"

Arabelle stared into her eyes, scared but unintimidated. "I wouldn't know, Quillian has never mentioned you," she stated coldly.

Shyla took a step back, clearly searching her mind for a response.

Arabelle continued, "I suppose I should be flattered you are so worried about my presence here, but honestly, I couldn't care less what you feel." She leant forward and smiled. "I guess Quillian and I have that in common," she added.

Shyla shoved her away. "Don't get too cocky little girl. Remember your place. You are food sweetheart, just his food."

Arabelle was unfazed. "So, I am something he needs to survive," she replied. "I have a purpose then, a very important purpose. Um what's your purpose... darling?"

The realisation of how dispensable she was, hit Shyla hard. All her insecurities and mediocre exchanges with Quillian were suddenly very apparent. She stared at the threat before her. Furious at Arabelles audacity but admittedly impressed by her gutsiness.

"I wasn't going to do this, but I think I have someone you should meet," she said confidently.

Arabelle nodded and smiled, she knew she had hit a nerve and made a mental note of her enemy's weakness. "Sure, I'm always ready to make new friends." Her body tensed ready for a fight.

Shyla smirked, "oh, this is not a new friend, this is an old friend."

Arabelle swallowed hard as she stood waiting, her mind raced with anticipation, pondering the potential identity of the person about to walk through the door. Throughout her life, she had known a lot of people, some friends, some enemies, but none of them possessed the capability to casually stroll into the office within the Hemovitalist compound.

The door slowly opened.

Arabelle stood frozen, her gaze fixed on the figure before her. The mere sight of whom sent a surge of bewilderment through her. Countless questions raced through her mind, yet her voice hesitated to articulate them. Finally breaking the silence, she managed to utter, "Madlyn? How on Earth..."

Madlyn stepped forward. Her expression betrayed her shame, but her body showed no signs of injury. Her weary smile, though gentle, sliced through Arabelle's heart like a knife. "Belle, believe me, this isn't what it looks like."

Shyla was in her element. "Unless what it looks like is, your little friend here has come to collect payment for giving me the location of Uronga."

Arabelle could not take her eyes off Madlyn as Shyla continued, "and all your kinship will be captured and Quillian and I are going to wine and dine on them for years to come. The end."

Arabelle's gaze remained fixed on Madlyn's face, unwavering and intent. Madlyn appeared guilty, and yet Arabelle found herself unable to fully grasp the reasons behind her clear remorse.

The moment remained in perplexity until Madlyn finally spoke.

"It's true, I had a meeting with this woman, but belle you have to believe me, I did not know what it was about. Morrison arranged it and I thought he had made a truce, he had the vaccine ... he said we will be saved, he was too old to travel and I offered, well he kinda, I mean he said I had to do it." Her ramblings stopped and she sternly looked at Arabelles betrayed face.

Madlyn took a deep breath. "You know me Arabelle, am I capable of this?"

Arabelle looked away. "You are here Mads, you are standing here, with that woman."

Madlyn was determined and unwavering in her stance. "Arabelle, Am...I... Capable... of this!?"

Arabelles mind meticulously sifted through a lifetime of memories for any trace that could point towards Madlyn's involvement in the unfolding drama. Madlyn, her symbol of trust and loyalty, now under Arabelle scrutinizing gaze as doubts crept into the corners of her mind. Each thought seemed to amplify the echoes of past conversations, emphasizing the genuine warmth that they had for each other, the endless examples of Madlyn's kind gestures. The laughter, the genuine belly aching laughter. Saving each other from a life of pain, delivering each other to the sanctuary of friendship.

The memories of Morrison's secretive laboratory resurfaced, the sterile scent of chemicals and the low hum of mysterious machinery haunting her recollection. She vividly recalled the cryptic nature of his discourse, the carefully chosen words that hinted at a mind adept at weaving complex plots. The room seemed to pulse with an unsettling energy, a silent acknowledgment of the potential deviousness lurking beneath the surface. As Arabelle pieced together the fragments of her thoughts the puzzle seemed to align, and the kind-hearted Madlyn, with her ever-obliging nature, emerged as a pawn in Morrison's calculated game.

Shyla laughed at Arabelles contemplative stare. "Look at you trying to figure it all out, what an idiot you are." she turned to Madlyn. "And you, you power hungry fool, I heard about the BioBot attack, Uronga is no more, and our deal is off."

In the crucial moment just before Arabelle could fully grasp Shyla's presence or pass judgment, a sharp, unmistakable crack pierced the air, emanating from Madlyn. The sound, a visceral snap of violence, conveyed the brutal impact of a blade penetrating flesh and grazing the shallow barrier of a chest plate. Snap after snap, the macabre rhythm of multiple wounds unfolded in rapid succession, a grim tempo that momentarily paralysed Arabelle's emotions.

In the blink of an eye, guided by an instinct too swift for conscious thought, Arabelle sprang into action. The source of the ominous sound crystallised in her mind. Madlyn, the unsuspecting victim, and Shyla, the aggressor armed with a large letter opener.

Without hesitation, Arabelle seized a weighted object from the nearby desk, its cold familiarity grounding her in the urgency of the moment. With practiced precision, she hurled the makeshift projectile towards Shyla, the force behind it generating a sharp crack upon impact. As the projectile connected with its target, a moment of realisation swept over Arabelle like a sickening tidal wave. Madlyn, it seemed, had become an unwitting casualty in Arabelle's desperate attempt to intervene.

The lingering resonance of the impact filled the air, a chilling foreshadowing of the unintended consequences unfolding. Both women crumpled to the unforgiving floor, each bearing the scars of this sudden eruption of violence.

Shyla holding onto life, despite her injuries, gathered herself for a hastily retreat.

Arabelle, now with multiple wounds etched into her heart, lay vulnerable to the cruel twist of fate.

Madlyn, with a jagged tear in the fabric of her flesh revealing a glimpse of the underlying anatomy, bore the weight of a pulsating, crimson crown on her head, where her blood was welling.

"No!" Arabelle's cry echoed through the room, a desperate exclamation, as she rushed to be by Madlyn's side.

"I'm so sorry, I'm so sorry," she kept repeating as she knelt next to Madlyn, holding her weakening hands and wiping away her tears. "I'm so sorry."

Shyla crawled desperately toward the door, summoning all her hemovitalist strength to resist the pull of death. Arabelle, ignored her escapee, Madlyn was all that mattered now.

Time seemed to slow, as though the universe was acknowledging the sacredness of their farewell.

"Mad, you're not alone," Arabelle whispers, her voice quivering. "I'll be here with you until the very end."

Madlyn's eyes, brimming with love and gratitude, locked onto Arabelle's. "I know you will; you always have been."

As Madlyn's hand grew colder and her breaths shallower, a heavy silence settled over the room. Arabelle could see the pain etched on her best friend's face, yet also saw an unselfish acceptance and tranquillity. She pressed her lips to Madlyn's bloodied forehead, a bittersweet kiss laden with affection and sorrow.

"I know you weren't capable of this, I know Mad. I know you aren't capable of this," Arabelle sobs.

Madlyn closed her eyes and smiled. A smile that seemed to capture the lifelong memories of a devoted friendship filled with respect and admiration. She looked so peaceful, so happy, and for the briefest of moments, Arabelle dared to believe her friend's death might not happen.

But happen it did.

Chapter Twenty-Eight

QUILLIAN'S GAZE REMAINED on the disarray before him, the sight so perplexing that he had to take a moment to process what he was seeing.

The office, which was once a sanctuary for their lovemaking, had now been completely transformed into a scene of crime, where the room itself served as a silent observer to the disturbing aftermath of a murder.

The silence within the space spoke volumes, and Quillian hesitated to probe Arabelle for the details. He instinctively knew words were better left unsaid.

Quillian, sitting beside Arabelle, observed the grief and pain engraved into her face, patiently waiting for the best moment when he could offer words, no matter how feeble, to provide some semblance of comfort.

Arabelle shifted her gaze towards Quillian, the pools of tears in her eyes rapidly drying as grief underwent a swift metamorphosis into seething anger. "Did you fucking know about this?"

"No! how could I know about this!." he replied firmly.

"Well let me fill you in shall I, your good mate the red head, has negotiated the surrender of my kinship to be your food source." Arabelle informed him.

"What! I knew nothing of that. It's not how we do things, certainly not how I operate," he retorted.

"You need a food source though," she spat back.

Quillian shook his head "We need volunteers to provide sustenance,"

"Oh okay, and how do you get the volunteers to sacrifice themselves?" She returned fire immediately.

Quillian remained calm. It was a question he had heard many times before: "It's hardly a sacrifice. They get food, shelter. They get to belong to a safe and advance community. We treat them well and we only take what we need."

Arabelle was silent and Quillian sensed he was finally connecting with her.

He continued. "If we had more stock... more volunteers than we would take less and less from each one. It's just math. We could only take a small amount from each person maybe once a month. The rest of the time they live a happy life doing what they wanted within the confines of this community."

Arabelle nodded her head. "Within the confines ... why do they have to be trapped here?"

"It's not being trapped. It's being protected. If the BioBots get you, you are bled dry. So, this is a far better option,." He replied.

"Why does certain death, or being a blood slave, have to be my only two options?" Arabelle asked rhetorically.

The energy between the two lovers underwent a dramatic shift, turning them into instant enemies in an intense exchange, each advocating for their own survival.

Quillian crafted a compelling argument that unfolded gradually, revealing the reality of her life before Arabelle's eyes.

"Belle, listen to me. As a hemovitalist we rely on fresh blood daily, maybe every two days. If we go longer than 4 days, we become weak, we start to die. After a month, we are pretty much useless. Our blood dies, coagulates, thickens, like our body is trying to survive with glue in its veins,"

Arabelle understood Hemoes required blood, but hearing one articulate their plight was more enlightening than anything she had read.

"Can't you use some other blood?" she asked.

"Each species has distinct blood types and molecular structures, including antigens, which play a crucial role in determining compatibility for blood use. Trust me, we have tried. The results were..."

Quillian's mind replayed haunting images of his comrades in agony. The memories, so vivid, still played in his mind. Scenes of their slow, torturous demise, each passing day marked by escalating suffering.

He continued, "the immune system of humans is designed to recognise and attack foreign substances, and this includes blood from other species."

"Human blood or death, they are your two choices," she confirmed.

"You see Belle, you aren't the only one who has to choose between two evils."

Quillian's fingers traced the invisible thread of a timeline, emphasising a critical point—human blood, a fleeting lifeline, could only be stored for a mere forty-five days. As he spoke his words, Arabelle felt the weight of the truth settling in the room.

It wasn't just a matter of survival; it was a battle with the delicate nature of mortality.

An unspoken understanding passed between them, creating an intense sense of connection. Their destinies were now intertwined, bound by the pulsating rhythm of life coursing through their veins. Quillian's conviction, palpable with his fear, spoke of a symbiotic dependence.

Arabelle tried to deal with the evolving dynamics of their alliance. The choice ahead loomed large: embrace the fragile partnership, a historical longshot, or face the imminent reality of dual adversaries. A world she knew well and wanted to avoid. However, Arabelle couldn't escape the undeniable truth—the fragility of their existence now bound them together, and the decisions made would impact others through the intertwined connections of their shared lives.

The full weight of Quillian's argument settled upon Arabelle's shoulders. She raised her hand, signalling for him to stop speaking. She had made the choice between having two enemies or having one enemy.

"I have a proposition." Arabelle sounded defeated but optimistic. "I know the location of a BioBot factory. If you help us to get in and destroy it, then you can take all the blood they have already harvested."

Quillian struggled to contain his excitement, his eager gaze betraying his intense fascination.

"And the humans?" he asked.

"Off limits!" Arabelle sternly replies.

Quillian sighs, "what if?"

"No!"

Quillian shot her a gaze that was both stern and playful, silently conveying, 'Hold on a minute, you feisty minx.'

Arabelle responded with a crafted look, a feigned expression of defeat that communicated, 'I'm listening,' in a playful yet attentive manner.

Quillian grinned at their chemistry, now he was getting somewhere. "What if I explained our situation and what we had to offer, and then just accepted volunteers?"

Arabelle pierced her lips in thought. "No coercion, no pressure, no bullshit," she replied. "You tell them the facts and they make up their own minds?"

"Yes!" Quillian excitedly replies.

"And you accept their decision?"

"Yes,"

"Regardless of what they decide?"

"Yes,"

"And at any point, they are free to leave?"

"Yes,"

"For any reason, at any time, they can go. No questions, no restraint?"

"Yes."

Arabelle looked at this man she hardly known. Sex was one thing. Trusting him in this moment, with the lives of others, was another. He had done nothing to give her doubts of his integrity, and the enticing prospect of saving those trapped in the pumping factory served as a dangling carrot in this tempting gamble.

She held out her hand, and with a firm handshake, the deal was made.

Arabelle looked around the room, surveying the aftermath.

"What about this?" she queried, her eyes gesturing to the chaotic scene.

"I have people," Quillian responded succinctly.

"People?" Arabelle interrupted, waving off any further explanations. "I don't want to know," she declared.

Quillian took her hand. "She will be looked after and laid to rest respectfully," he assured.

Arabelle drew in a deep breath, gathering her grief and casting aside any lingering remorse.

Life, relentless, surges forward. Despite feeling the weight of responsibility of her handshake deal, her eyes filled with a firm determination. With a solemn dedication to her best friend's memory, she steeled herself for the challenge ahead. There were countless lives in need of saving, and she intended to do so with unwavering fortitude in Madlyn's name.

Arabelle looked at Quillian "Pack some supplies," she said sternly.

"For what?"

"I need you to come with me, I have an idea and we have a long walk ahead."

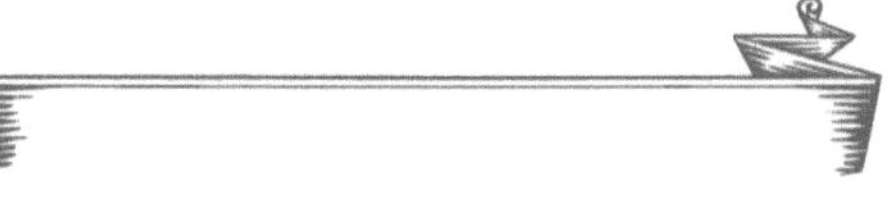

Chapter Twenty-Nine

Anarrow trail, flanked by ferns and moss-covered rocks, guided them to the cave entrance. The ground beneath yielded softly underfoot, layered with damp decaying leaves that served as a natural carpet, muffling their footsteps. Quillian felt a strong sense of unease as he and Arabelle neared the humans' cave campsite, fully aware that they were entering hostile territory. The fate of Quillian's integration into the kinship relied on the efforts of a single woman.

The symphony of the rainforest from unseen creatures, the melodic trill of tiny birds, and the soothing murmur of a nearby stream set his mind at ease. Nothing bad could happen in a place like this. He took in his beautiful natural surroundings. His underground bunker, with its expensive trinkets and priceless pieces, didn't seem so luxurious anymore.

"Stop, who goes there?" a booming voice commanded.

"It's Arabelle, and I love that you finally decided to post some guards. It's about time."

"The tall, bulky man appeared unamused by Arabelle's quip. "Who is that?" he demanded, pointing at Quillian.

"He's with me," she replied.

"Who is he?" the guard repeated.

"He's a Hemovitalist, and he could rip you apart. So, shut up and let us through," Arabelle asserted.

Quillian looked shocked at Arabelle's response. "She is joking! I wouldn't do that," he said with a smile. The guard didn't know which one was more sincere.

Arabelle approached the guard and rested her hand on his shoulder. "He's helping me out. I trust him, so can you. Listen, I have a plan that could save thousands of people. Please?"

The campsite itself exuded a harmonious blend of rustic charm and thoughtful organisation. Makeshift tents, blending with the earth-toned colours of the surroundings, stood strategically pitched in a cave's cavernous clearing. Each tent bore the marks of rainforest life, sprinkled with tiny droplets from the humidity that clung to the fabric like glistening diamonds in the filtered sunlight. Encircling the camp, a ring of stones embraced a central fire pit, its smoky aroma intertwining with the natural scents of the rainforest. Weathered logs and large rocks served as impromptu seating, beckoning all to gather around the flickering flames as twilight painted the sky in hues of orange and purple.

"Wow, you established this place so quickly," Quillian observed.

"We are used to it," Arabelle replied.

The Kinship had gathered in a smaller area, their murmurs filling the air. As soon as Arabelle approached, they instinctively formed a semicircle around her and her attractive companion.

"This is Quillian, my Hemovitalist friend," she announced to the group.

An explosion of protest erupted from the crowd. Their leader had brought the enemy directly to their camp. The group started voicing their dissent with a rising tide of louder and louder chatter.

"Shut up!" she yelled. "Do you really think I would have brought a Hemo to our home if it wasn't for something important?"

The group fell silent, all eyes focused and waiting. Eager to hear the reason behind this invasion of not only their privacy but their safety.

Arabelle leapt into leadership mode as she skilfully unravelled the details of the blood issue, weaving a chronicle that exposed its hidden layers. Her conversation with Quillian unfolded like a captivating tale in the past tense, with each detail laden with profound significance.

Instead of just stating her case, Arabelle painted a vivid picture of the humans' crucial role. She gestured towards the surrounding forest, mapping out the plan with sweeping motions, allowing each member of the kinship to envision their part in the unfolding drama.

The air buzzed with anticipation as she described the unique contribution each individual could make, and the potential benefits hung in the collective imagination like ripe fruit waiting to be plucked.

Amidst her sermon, Arabelle's charisma commanded the spotlight. Her gestures transformed into a graceful dance, while her words composed a resonant melody that touched every member of the kinship. She conveyed the essence of freedom not through loud proclamations but with subtle nods and encouraging glances directed at each listener. The atmosphere underwent a transformation, evolving into a collective of shared understanding and voluntary commitment.

No longer a speaker but a storyteller, Arabelle's reassuring presence worked its enchantment. The kinship, swept up in the narrative, found themselves not just in agreement but eager participants in the unfolding saga. The once abstract proposal became a living, breathing entity, embraced not by just consent but by the genuine enthusiasm of those who had seen the promise of a shared adventure.

Quillian, silent and admiring, stood back, captivated by the effortless grace with which his gorgeous lover commanded the audience. A born leader, she was a valuable asset to her kin, and he couldn't help but marvel at the innate strength she exuded. As he observed her in action, a pang of longing gripped Quillian.

If only she were a Hemo, he thought, envisioning a scenario where her allegiance had been with him from the start. In that alternate reality, he wouldn't find himself in the position of pleading for help; instead, he could have been orchestrating the human conquest necessary to secure his group's needs.

As the sun dipped below the horizon, the cave's entrance bathed in warm, amber light revealed textured walls, stalactites, and stalagmites casting tiny shadows. The group settled into their makeshift headquarters; the air was alive with eager chatter about the lives they were about to change. Conversations buzzed with anticipation as they envisioned the families, friends, and potential new connections they hoped to rescue.

Quillian, however, struggled to match their enthusiasm. His attempts to join the lively discussions about humans as cherished companions, not just resources, felt awkward and forced.

As Arabelle made her way out of the cave, a mixture of determination and concern etched across her face, Quillian debated following her.

There was a heavy silence in the air, as if burdened by the weight of a personal matter left unaddressed. Instead, he hesitated, observing from a distance, torn between curiosity and the need to respect her privacy. Patience became his silent companion as he awaited her return.

Arabelle approached Morrison with measured steps, taking her time to scrutinise his face, observe his body language, and attempt to decipher any signs of guilt. He maintained the appearance of innocence, blending into the crowd and exchanging pleasantries in the outdoor area. This ability only deepened Arabelle's conviction of his guilt; any ordinary person would have acknowledged her presence by now.

"Morrison, can I have a word?" she called over to him.

Morrison nodded and walked in her direction, avoiding eye contact.

"I heard about Madlyn. I'm sorry," he said flatly, his voice lacking any trace of emotion, as he trailed behind Arabelle to a more secluded spot.

Arabelle turned to face him, the rage inside her not manifesting in her face.

"Why are you sorry?" she asked quietly.

Morrison shrugged. "Well, she was your friend and all."

Arabelle could no longer feign ignorance. Uninterested in games and unafraid to express her emotions, she got straight to the point.

"Morrison, Madlyn said you sent her to the Hemoes to discuss a vaccine. She claimed you orchestrated the whole thing and convinced her to go in your place."

Morrison did not appear shocked by the accusation; instead, he bowed his head.

"I know. I've been thinking about how that could have been me."

Arabelle did a double-take. "Wait, so you admit it was you?"

Morrison rolled his eyes. "Look, woman, I'm too old for this. Yes, it was me. Yes, I said I had the vaccine. I didn't test it, of course, and yes, I was negotiating with the Hemoes, but Madlyn approached me. She knew what I was up to, and I guess she wanted in on it. So, of course, I accepted her help."

Arabelle had no words to offer, just a stunned look on her face.

Morrison continued. "You know what she is like—sorry, what she was like—sweet, helpful Maddy. So, of course, I wasn't going to say no; it makes my job easier."

Arabelle's fists clenched as she moved closer to Morrison, a menacing glare fixed on her target. Her movements were deliberate, each step echoing a silent countdown.

"Oh come on Arabelle, people die every day around here. What are you so angry about?" The confusion on Morrison's face shattered by the sudden snap of a bone meeting its unfortunate fate. A swift kick to his leg followed by a sickening crunching sound, as he crumpled to the ground, a tortured groan escaping from his clenched teeth.

"What the fuck bitch, I didn't kill her, I was trying to help." Morrison screamed.

Arabelle lifted her leg and slammed her foot down hard onto his other leg, instantly disabling him. The sharp, acrid scent of pain permeated the air, joining the metallic tang of spilled blood.

Morrison let out a howl of pain.

"No! I'm sorry, please stop," he wailed.

Arabelle stood over him, the stillness of the moment only disturbed by muffled whimpering.

The message was simple—two kneecaps shattered. Revenge had been taken, and he would die slowly, for a merciful death was too good for him.

Arabelle strode back into the cave with a calm confidence. She positioned herself beside a visibly bored Quillian, intertwining her fingers with his, an emblem of trust unveiled for the entire kinship to witness.

"Morrison is guilty of treason and murder," she declared with unwavering authority. "I have administered his punishment."

The stunned faces before her dared not challenge her authoritative judgment. Eyes averted, they agreed.

"Anyone who helps him," she proclaimed, her intense stare unwavering, "will answer to me."

Chapter Thirty

Engaging in an assault under the glaring sunlight might have seemed like a perilous tactic, but within its audacity lay an undeniable genuineness. The BioBots, typically engrossed in their harvesting operations during the day, roamed the surrounding areas, capturing unsuspecting humans and venturing farther afield, leaving their factory vulnerable for extended periods.

As Arabelle stealthily crawled across the velvety green grass of the paddock toward their target, the smell of grass transported her to a time long before the war. A mental landscape emerged, featuring green paddocks, grazing sheep, a radiant sun, and a gentle breeze that whisked away stress into the encircling mountains. Closing her eyes, she embraced the memory, momentarily escaping the harsh realities of the present.

"You ready for this" Quillian asked nervously. Arabelle confidently nodded.

Turning her attention to the assembled band of misfits that followed her. A motley crew comprising both Humans and Hemoes, with a common thread of mostly untrained warriors, driven by good intentions and resolute spirits. She knew not all would emerge unscathed, but hope that the lives saved would outweigh the sacrifices, rendering the losses somehow worthwhile.

Gaining entry into the factory proved astonishingly straightforward. Snipping a few wires and delivering a frustrated punch to the door was all it took to secure access. Initially, Arabelle harboured a momentary concern about potential traps, but then she recalled the BioBots' low opinion of humans. It struck her that they likely underestimated humans, presuming an over thought-out elaborate plan of attack rather than a basic brute force assault on the door.

The factory sprawled like a confusing maze, its corridors tangled with doors and misleading passages. The lack of any discernible signs or functional design was clear in the haphazard construction of rooms, and the machinery and piping scattered awkwardly in spare areas.

The rescue team navigated through the building, pulling on doors and cautiously peering around corners. The mission felt more like a disorganised tourist tour than a military operation.

Arabelle trailed behind Quillian, shielded by his imposing figure and superior strength, although she couldn't shake the irritation of not being in her usual lead position.

Amid the meandering group, a quiet yet forceful voice called out, "Here!" The team turned to find an opened door, and the fearful face of a man beckoning from within. He gestured towards the open entrance as Arabelle moved in to get a closer look.

As Arabelle cautiously peered into the room, her eyes grew wide with astonishment upon seeing a smaller group of humans huddled together, their faces displaying a mix of fear and anticipation etched deeply into their expressions. The rescue mission had reached a critical juncture, and Arabelle knew that their actions in the next few moments could shape the fate of these people and the entire struggle of the Hemovitalists.

As the rescue team gathered in the cramped room, their attention focused on the smaller group of humans huddled in fear, a revelation unfolded behind them. A larger group of humans, already processed, stood in rows of one hundred capsules. Tubes connected to these capsules contained one hundred bodies in various states of repose, appearing surprisingly well-preserved given the circumstances. It seemed they had not been draining for too long, suggesting a recent capture or a more efficient extraction process.

As Arabelle looked around, she couldn't help but be amazed by the unexpectedly large size of the group before her. One hundred and ten humans had already been discovered, and they hadn't even reached the midway point of their search. Hope surged within her, fuelling a renewed determination to save as many lives as possible.

However, the optimism was tempered by the harsh reality of their situation. The factory, with its cold and sterile environment, reminded her of the dehumanising practices of the Hemovitalists. The rescue mission had only just begun, and the challenges ahead seemed more daunting than ever.

Arabelle turned her gaze back to the smaller group, a mix of gratitude and trepidation in their eyes. Contemplating the way forward, she felt the immense weight of responsibility. Fully aware that each choice she made would play a pivotal role in shaping the destiny of the imprisoned souls and in the ongoing fight against those who wished to take advantage of them.

"Here," another voice echoed through the confined space, drawing the attention of the rescue team to an opening behind which stood a large sliding glass door. Quillian approached, peering through the glass to witness a staggering sight: thousands of clear capsules containing bodies. Some appeared beyond saving, but the majority seemed viable for Quillian's collection.

"The motherload," he loudly whispered to Arabelle as she approached, her eyes filling with tears as she beheld more humans than she had ever seen in her lifetime. The scale of the horror unfolding before her, and the weight of the situation pressed heavily on her heart.

Unable to contain her anguish, Arabelle immediately started banging on the glass, her desperation clear. "Shhh," Quillian shouted, attempting to maintain some semblance of control.

Ignoring his command, Arabelle continued to claw at the control panel, desperately trying to trigger the opening of the door. Unbeknownst to her, the glass was impenetrable, and the door was sealed shut. Not even a BioBot could open it. The automated process took care of the disposal and renewal of bodies, and regardless of how hard anyone tried, no one would be getting into that room unless they were captured, processed, and sent for draining.

Quillian watched Arabelle's futile efforts, torn between the grim reality of their situation and the ruthless pragmatism that had driven him to this point. The rescue mission had reached a critical impasse, and the fate of those within the capsules hung in the balance, their futures dictated by the merciless mechanisms of the factory.

A small, ominous red light blinked in the softly lit hallway, catching the attention of a keen-eyed member of the rescue team. The significance of the flashing light sent a shiver down her spine. "They are coming," she announced, her voice filled with urgency.

In response to the warning, the team swiftly gathered, their focus shifting from the glass door to the imminent threat that loomed. The room grew silent, and the tension in the air became more pronounced as they began to fully understand the seriousness of the situation. The Tourist Tour was over.

One member, a quick thinker, sprinted to the end of the hallway, disappearing momentarily. She returned minutes later, a panicked look etched across her face.

"We've got to get out of here!" she yelled, her voice echoing through the sterile corridors.

Arabelle, still reeling from the emotional impact of the motherload room, redirected her attention to the urgent call for escape. The relentless banging on the doors had triggered the attention of the protection Bots, the automated guardians of the factory. A large group of them was now advancing towards the rescue team, responding to the perceived threat.

A low mechanical growl echoed through the corridor, sending chills down their backs. A young man raised a hand, signalling for the group to halt. They pressed themselves against the walls, blending into the shadows as a horde of BioBots emerged from the darkness ahead.

THE BIOBOTS WERE A twisted fusion of flesh and machine, older obsolete models left behind for defence but hardly suited for the job. The young man's heart raced as he surveyed their numbers, knowing that they were outnumbered. The air was thick with the scent of oil and metal, and the only light came from the flickering fluorescent bulbs overhead.

Without hesitation, the BioBots launched their attack, charging forward with speed. The young man and his comrades sprang into action, meeting the onslaught head-on with a fierce determination. Blades clashed against metal, erupted in deafening bursts, and screams echoed through the corridors as the two sides clashed in a chaotic frenzy.

The young man fought with the skill of a seasoned warrior, his movements fluid and precise as he dispatched the old BioBots with lethal efficiency. His companions, Humans and Hemoes, fought bravely beside him, each one holding their ground against the persistent tide of their mechanical enemies.

In the midst of the anarchy, a brilliant flash illuminated the corridor as one of the Hemoes unleashed a homemade Electromagnetic Pulse device. The BioBots convulsed and spasmed, their artificial systems temporarily disabled. Seizing the opportunity, the Humans pressed their advantage, delivering decisive blows to the vulnerable machines.

"It worked! It could have exploded and killed us all," The Hemo announced proudly after the fact.

"Got any more?" the young man yelled across the conflict.

"Nope, prototype," the Hemo yelled back.

A large mechanical behemoth appeared through the bedlam. It's cold, metallic gaze fixated on its targets. A silent understanding passed between the Human and Hemo as they shared a brief nod, acknowledging the need of the situation. Without a word, they seamlessly synchronised their movements, moving in tandem to outmanoeuvre the Bot.

The young man took on the role of a distracter, cleverly dodging the BioBots powerful strikes while leading it on a calculated walk through the confusion of conflict. The Hemo seized the opportunity, strategically positioning himself for a precision attack. As the BioBot's attention remained fixated on the agile evader, the Hemo launched a coordinated assault, exploiting vulnerabilities in the machine's design.

The duo moved with a fluidity, they weaved between towering stacks of crates and debris using the environment to their advantage. With a well-timed distraction, the human lured the BioBot into a vulnerable position, while the Hemo unleashed a barrage of strikes targeting crucial joints and circuitry.

The BioBot, caught off guard by the double assault, faltered under the combined pressure. Its movements became erratic, its responses delayed. The Hemo-Human partnership seized the moment, exploiting the biomechanical weaknesses until, with a final, coordinated strike, they brought the machine to a halt.

The two exchanged a triumphant glance and returned to battle.

Slowly but surely, the tide of battle began to turn. With each BioBot that fell, the new Human-Hemo coalition gained ground, pushing their attackers back with relentless determination. The factory corridors became a combat zone strewn with the wreckage of both human and machine, great casualties on both sides, and then, finally, it was over.

The last of the BioBots lay in ruins at their feet, the young man and his team stood amidst the wreckage, battered, and bloodied, but victorious.

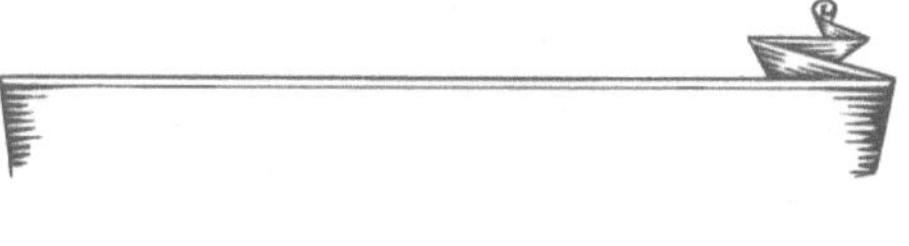

Chapter Thirty-One

THE GROUP, NOW FUELLED by a newfound sense of comradery, began to move with purpose. The corridors, once echoing with desperate attempts to save lives, now reverberated with the hurried footsteps of those fighting for their own survival.

The red light continued its ominous pulse, casting an eerie glow over the scene as the rescuers navigated through the convoluted passages, seeking an escape route from a possible second encroaching threat.

Arabelle, torn between the desire to save lives and the immediate need for self-preservation, led her team with determination. With the possible confrontation with more protection Bots, the mission, already perilous, became even more complex, altering the rescue operation into a race against time and cutting-edge technology right in the heart of the BioBot's stronghold.

The more Quillian and Arabelle tried to break through the sliding door, the more apparent Quillian's frustration became.

"We aren't going to get in," he declared, his voice filled with a sense of urgency. "It's impossible, let's go!"

Arabelle, equally determined, couldn't tear herself away from the unyielding barrier. She kept trying to break through, her hands pounding on the transparent surface. "You go back and take as much blood as you can. I'm going to keep trying this," she ordered, her tone sharp with desperation.

Quillian didn't step away, his determination to stop her unshaken. "It's pointless. We need to get the people, take as many as we can," he insisted, a sense of practicality in his voice.

Arabelle reluctantly nodded, frustration turning into resignation as she furiously wrenched at the door.

Quillian grabbed her Arabelles arm. "I'll take twenty-five percent and you take the rest," he suggested, his words hanging in the tense air as he continued to pull at her.

Arabelle paused, her movements freezing as she absorbed the weight of his statement. "Take?" she repeated, a mix of confusion and disbelief in her eyes. The realisation dawned on her, and she met Quillian's gaze with a mix of shock and understanding. The gravity of their situation became all too clear.

The air felt heavy with the weight of Quillian's suggestion, as if the changing circumstances were pressing down on them both.

"Yes, take," he reiterated, his tone holding a sense of urgency and a tinge of frustration.

"The parameters of our agreement have changed. The blood stores will barely sustain us for a week, and we don't even know how old they are."

Arabelle's disbelief deepened, and a sense of betrayal washed over her. The man she had trusted with their survival was suggesting a course of action that went against everything she believed in. She took a step back, distancing herself from the door and Quillian. The reality of their predicament sank in, and she felt a surge of panic and helplessness.

"Take them?" she repeated

"It's different now, I have to take," he replied.

She pondered for a moment, desperately searching for an alternative plan. Could she somehow save the smaller group, protect them from the Hemovitalist, and find a way to outsmart their adversaries? The odds were against her, and she knew it. She couldn't agree to Quillian's terms, but she needed a solution, a way to turn the tables without sacrificing the principles that defined her.

In the tense silence that followed, Arabelle locked eyes with Quillian, a mixture of defiance and determination in her gaze. The struggle between survival and morality played out on her face as she braced herself for the next move in this deadly game.

Arabelle ceased her attempts at opening the door, her determination firm.

"We save the smaller group," she declared to Quillian, her voice unwavering. "You get volunteers, as per our agreement."

Quillian, though angered by her defiance, masked his emotions. He knew he couldn't afford to let her see his frustration; negotiation was crucial, especially in the heat of battle.

"I get to take and bleed all of them, and will release the ones who don't volunteer to stay on," he proposed calmly, trying to maintained control over the situation.

Unable to comprehend the moral dilemma they were facing, Arabelle shook her head in disbelief, her mind racing.

"Why are we even talking about this?" she yelled, frustration and disbelief obvious in her voice.

Quillian remained silent for a moment before responding, his tone cold and detached.

"Get them all out, and we can talk terms after," he replied, his focus solely on the immediate task at hand.

Arabelle chose to ignore his heartless language, recognising that saving a smaller group was better than nothing. She needed to work on Quillian, appeal to whatever charm she had over him, and eventually guide him towards a more humane course of action.

For now, the priority was rescuing the people. She pondered on a plan to keep them safe within the Hemovitalist compound until she could establish a more secure and permanent sanctuary for the humans. The battle for both survival and morality raged on, and Arabelle was determined to navigate it with cunning and compassion.

Quillian, with an air of triumph, turned towards his loyal army, a sense of pride evident in his demeanour. Making a series of hand gestures, he directed his well-disciplined soldiers into action. The group moved with a synchronised precision that sent shivers down Arabelle's spine. It was as if they had rehearsed this scenario countless times before, an unsettling display of organisation and efficiency.

As Quillian's army surged towards the room holding the smaller group of humans, Arabelle couldn't shake the feeling of unease. The speed and discipline with which they moved hinted at a level of experience that surpassed her understanding. She watched as they approached the door, ready to carry out their leader's orders.

Quillian waved at a small team, signalling them for a specific task. And, in the midst of his commanding gestures, barked out orders to his team with a commanding tone.

"Get the blood bags!" he commanded loudly, not realising the derogatory term he had just used for the humans.

As the words were spoken, they seemed to linger in the air, creating an uncomfortable stillness. Arabelle winced at the dehumanising language, her eyes narrowing as she observed the situation unfolding. The slip revealed more about Quillian's mindset and the perilous nature of their alliance. She knew she had to find a way to change the course of events, to ensure not just the physical safety of the smaller group but also their dignity and humanity.

Arabelle gathered her Kinship, a calm urgency in her voice.

"Let's get out of here; our Hemo friends have got this," she declared with a confident smile, attempting to reassure her Kin.

She looked each member in the eye, conveying both determination and trust.

"You all know where to meet up. Now, go, go, go!"

Her words were a rallying cry, urged them to move swiftly and with purpose. Arabelle watched them go, her heart filled with a blend of concern for their safety and confidence in their abilities.

With one last glance over her shoulder, she joined the flowing stream of her Kinship, weaving through corridors to safety.

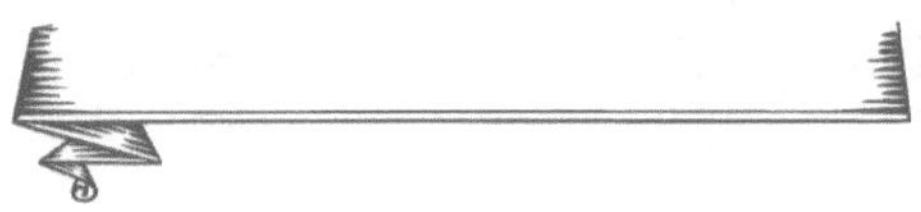

Chapter Thirty-Two

As Roland surveyed the medical centre, its sterile walls and hushed atmosphere felt eerily vacant, save for a lone occupant. Shyla, lying motionless in her bed, was clothed only in bloodied bandages wrapped tightly around her chest, the stark evidence of her most recent battle with humans.

"Please," Roland implored, a note of desperation in his voice.

Turning her eyes toward him, Shyla fixed him with a stern look.

"No. I don't want them in here. This isn't a charity case, and I will not be surrounded by humans while I am trying to recover."

Roland grappling with the conflict between his concern for Shyla's well-being and the stockpile of humans he had in the compound's common room. The medical equipment hummed softly in the background, a strange soundtrack to the emotional standoff unfolding within the sterile confines of the centre.

Despite the clinical environment, Roland felt a surge of empathy for Shyla, recognising the vulnerability beneath her stoic exterior. He pondered the delicate balance between respecting her wishes and ensuring others were being care for. The stark contrast between Shyla's solitary, bandaged form and the pristine, unoccupied beds around her underscored the selfishness she had chosen.

"As you wish," he conceded. Fully aware that, if given the option, he did not want Shyla as an enemy.

IT WAS OVERWHELMING, the common room had served as a communal haven, designated more for meetings and joyous celebrations rather than as a refugee camp. The floor was now a chaotic mess, with bed linen and bodies scattered about, each one at a different stage of undress. Some figures had exuded an air of strength, their expressions a mix of sullenness and fear, but their physical vigour had been clear.

There had been those who seemed as if they might not endure the night—fragile and malnourished. Their gaunt frames had spoken of prolonged hardship.

A sombre quiet had enveloped the space, devoid of the typical sounds that accompany such scenes. There had been no cries, no screams of pain; instead, a dense feeling of defeat hung in the air, heavy with the gravity of the situation.

Surrounded by the emotional scene, Roland moved with determination, carrying the burden of responsibility on his squared shoulders. The disarray surrounding him begged for order. A plea echoed in the tangled bed linen and the weary bodies strewn across the floor. Surrounded by the turmoil, Roland emerged as a leader, each of his actions silently vowing to bring back stability.

The desperate souls scattered throughout the room awaited a resolution, their eyes seeking reassurance. Roland, aware of the gravity of his task, could do nothing to reassure his human guests. The reality of their situation was clear to him. His words, as he addressed the guests, held a profound weight that went beyond their meaning. Each explanation, each attempt at reassurance, conveyed the unspoken truth, the stark reality. They would never leave this place.

He methodically scanned the room, his keen eyes performing a silent headcount.

As he looked at the tired faces of the individuals, their expressions of relief and exhaustion seemed to pass by unnoticed, failing to leave a lasting impression on his heart. Instead, Roland's mental faculties focused on a different calculus—one that revolved around the quantifiable metrics of survival. In his mind, the volume of blood per body, the intricacies of processing time, and the limitations of storage capacity took precedence over the emotional distinctions of the moment.

"Forty-eight," he muttered disapprovingly, a note of disappointment lacing his words. He couldn't help but express his frustration aloud, a reaction to the stark contrast between the number of humans they found and the meagre number of survivors they had managed to rescue.

Roland lamented the result, "Thousands, there were thousands ... and we've got forty-fucking-eight. How are we going to survive on forty fucking eight?"

Quillian swung open the door to his personal abode and cheerfully bounded into the space. Even though they had not emerged as triumphantly as hoped, he sensed the exhilaration of battle still coursing through his veins. With an affectionate gaze, he turned toward Arabelle. However, her expression did not mirror his emotions; instead, she appeared displeased.

Quillian wrinkled his forehead in thought. "You okay?"

"What the fuck was that?" She abruptly retorted.

"What the fuck was what?" Quillian responded, genuinely confused.

The conversation veered toward treacherous territories, Arabelle's eyes, once filled with adoration, clouded over with a shadow of conflict. The weight of a moral dilemma pressed upon her, tangible in the furrow of her brows and the tentativeness that lingered in the air.

The prospect of sacrificing her friends to a life of servitude hung heavy in her heart, and Quillian's demand had crossed an unspoken line.

Her body language shifted subtly, a tightening of the jaw and a subtle recoil, signalling her steadfast refusal. It wasn't just a matter of refusal; it was a deep-seated rejection of the concept itself.

The notion of surrendering her existence to nourish another's, represented, in her eyes, a form of enslavement. Arabelle responded instinctively rather than thoughtfully. The man standing before her, had transformed from a symbol of love into a representative of a group intent on destroying her kin. She aimed a punch at him, but his lightning-fast reflexes evaded contact.

Quillian did not appear shocked; deep in his heart, he knew her reaction would unfold just as it was now, he was expecting resistance.

"Belle, now come on. Think with your brain, not your heart. You know we all can't survive without some give and take."

Arabelle's hand moved slowly to her sword "So, we give, and you take?"

Quillian sighed audibly. "Oh, okay, so it is better you condemn all Hemovitalist to death? He huffed. "At least we can keep your kind alive."

"My kind?" she repeated. With that one statement, the differences between them were suddenly; very apparent.

Something unexpectedly saddened Arabelle. "Can't we co-exist?" she asked softly.

"Yes, we can make this work. We need your kind." Quillian replied as Arabelle grimaced at his continued reference to 'her kind.'

"I understand, but do we need you?" She questioned. "Do we need you to survive, or do we just need you to stop hunting us, and then we survive free?"

Quillian grew impatient, now was not the time to debate semantics. "Think about it, you can't defeat us, you can't team up with the BioBots, you basically have no choice, you need to pick a side and give that side what they want." He appeared troubled, his attempts to convey his thoughts with precision falling short of his intentions.

Clarity washed over Arabelle's life. The man she thought she could love, would never be her equal; instead, she would continually support him, tethered to his every need. Fleetingly, the notion of submitting and embracing her destiny crossed her mind. Yet, determining the fate of others was not a choice she could make.

Condemning survivors to a life no better than that of a dairy cow was a burden she couldn't bear. Her agreement with Quillian, like every Human-Hemo deal in history, had reached an impasse, and she understood the course of action she needed to take.

Arabelle nodded to herself. The path forward was clear. She had reached a decision.

She swung her sword at Quillian, slicing through his shirt and gently opening a thin line on his chest.

"I'm not going to fucking fight you," he responded through gritted teeth.

"I'm not going to fucking feed you," Arabelle replies.

"I can take what I want by force, you know this, can't you just be thankful that..." Quillian did not get to finish his sentence as Arabelle lunged at him again.

He grabbed the blade of her sword and wrenched it from her hands, throwing it on the ground with a brutal display of strength and willpower against the pain. A splash of blood flicked onto the floor as he stood, disregarding his injured hand, his gaze fixed on Arabelle.

"Don't make me kill you Arabelle ... at the very least it would be a waste of blood," he threatened.

Arabelle's petite frame stood in stark contrast to the bulk of her opponent, yet she fearlessly launched her attack. Fuelled by anger and a broken heart, she harnessed a power from within her very soul, embodying the strength of a man combined with the agility of a wild animal.

She was the first to strike.

They exchanged quick, powerful blows. Each move was met with a counter, a violent dance of punches and kicks. There was no wasted energy, no unnecessary flair. It was a brutal relentless sequence of hits, a contest of strength and skill. Fists and feet connected with precision; the lovers turned fighters, pushing each other to the limit.

The rhythm of the fight determined by the sound of impacts, the grunts of effort, and the occasional shuffle of footwork. No grand gestures, just the raw intensity of combat until one succumbed to the unrelenting assault.

Arabelle dropped to her knees, gasping for breath, and clutching her side in agony. It was clear to her that Quillian was not using his full power in the fight, as she could feel his restraint, yet she was almost at her end.

Quillian cautiously approached. She was a skilled combatant, and he refused to believe she was defeated.

"Belle, stop trying to be a hero. You are only a human. It's time to accept your place in the food chain. Please."

Suddenly and with remarkable agility, Arabelle executed a swift manoeuvre, smoothly transitioning to a controlled fall on her arms. Simultaneously, she snapped one leg forward, delivering a swift and targeted flick kick that found its mark squarely into Quillian's soft groin, leaving him temporarily incapacitated.

A moment was all she needed.

Arabelle instinctively executed a perfect commando roll, faultlessly traversing the floor to reach her trusty blade. With a swift and practiced motion, she secured the sword with both hands, rising to her feet. In a calculated and decisive move, she swung the blade with precision toward Quillian's exposed throat, flawlessly removing his head.

His lifeless body crumpled to the floor, succumbing almost instantaneously to the lethal strike. The severed head tumbled across the ground, eventually coming to rest at Arabelle's feet. She gazed down at his lifeless face. The captivating beauty of his green eyes still struck her. Even in death, they were mesmerizing.

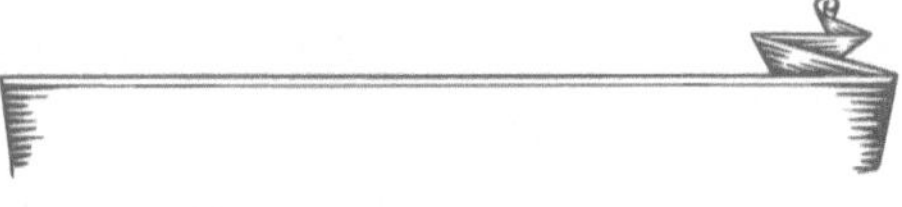

Chapter Thirty-Three

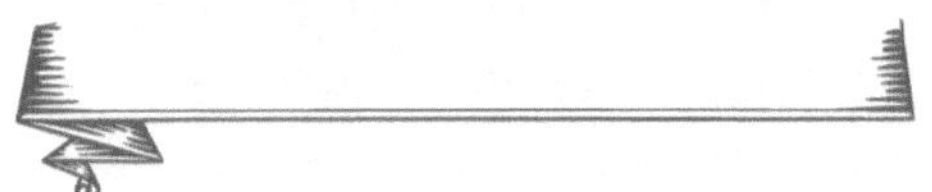

BENJAMIN GASPED FOR breath after the abrupt impact with the steel bed beneath him. The scenario of finding himself completely naked, trapped in a tube, was far from how he envisioned his final special forces mission would go.

He scanned the warehouse sized room. Too late to initiate a withdrawal.

A former member of the military, fuelled with bravado, he had eagerly volunteered for this mission. However, being in the present situation was an entirely different narrative. He felt helpless, and he felt scared, feelings that did not sit comfortably with him.

The title of 'the man who saved humanity' sounded appealing when initially pitched, but right now, the stark reality of becoming a human sacrifice weighed heavily on his mind.

"Hi, I'm Jenny." A cheerful but weak voice came from the pod beside him.

"What?" he gasped.

"You're in the juicing factory... don't worry, it doesn't hurt."

Benjamin could not be bothered with pleasantries. "I know where I am!" he snapped back.

He shifted uncomfortably and his discomfort grew as he noticed that with every passing minute, his body seemed to become heavier and heavier, as if a force-field were bearing down, pinning him to the steel bed beneath him. He tried to move; a sharp pain shot through his wrist. He noticed the cannula. He couldn't remember when it had been inserted but regardless, it was lodged deep, causing an incessant itch.

"Vigilance in Valour, Unity in Duty," he could think of no other words "Vigilance in Valour, Unity in Duty." Despite the flawless execution of the plan, a nagging feeling of dread persisted.

Benjamin turned his head towards the source of the voice he had heard earlier.

A naked woman. He wanted to turn away, but her emaciated body trapped his stare. She looked like death. A malnourished, drained corpse. It surprised him she could even speak.

"How long have you been here?" he asked.

"A while," she replied.

A surge of anger filled his body. This was supposed to be quick. They promised him he wouldn't suffer.

He looked beyond the never-ending rows of body filled capsules, his eyes searching for an exit. Not knowing that this room was one of a hundred others like it. Identical in layout. Identical in purpose. The entire building covering a square mile.

He tried to analyse the best extraction point. Benjamin had not yet accepted his fate. Weeks from now, he would. When he completed his mission and his body stopped producing blood faster than it was extracted, he would welcome death. But for now, he was resolute.

He felt the suction and saw his blood leave his body. Watching the red liquid flow through the transparent tube, tracing its path as it vanished into the floor. A moment of relief crossed his face as he smiled.

He wished he could see the Nanoquarks. He knew that his bloodstream was saturated with them, and it was a mega dose that had nearly proved fatal. However, there was only one chance to execute this operative successfully, and the goal was to guarantee a steady flow of Nanoquarks to neutralize as many BioBots as they could. It was a calculated risk.

Benjamin became angry again. Knowing they were there felt inadequate to the gravity of the situation. He stared at his blood, trying to see what could not be seen, he wanted to witness them infiltrating the system. He wanted the satisfaction.

"I'm going to kill every last one of these bastards and I'm taking this blood sucking farm down with them!" With a fierce battle cry, he unleashed all his fear.

Chapter Thirty-Four

WALKING AWAY FROM ARABELLE would be Byron's biggest challenge. A lifetime of admiration and protection, yet, on her insistence, he would have to leave her behind as he set off to build a new life in a world now unfamiliar to him. He held her close, trying to physically absorb her as they embraced for the last time. Inhaling deeply, he let her scent become a part of him. He knew she would be okay; he knew this was her wish, yet the pain of never seeing her again was killing him inside.

"Bye," he whispered as he pulled away from her embraced and walked towards Dalton.

Dalton smiled warmly at Arabelle, waving in a way that conveyed a "see you later" rather than a definitive "goodbye forever." Farewells were never his strong suit; they felt too permanent, leaving him with a lingering sense of sadness. He nodded in Byron's direction and chuckled knowingly, while Arabelle playfully raised her eyebrows in a suggestive double motion.

Dalton had never entertained living on his own. Hardly the warrior. He needed protection and Byron was the perfect solution, and great eye candy to boot. He would be nothing more than a friend, and Dalton had accepted this. Platonic friendship, unrequited love. After a while, it all felt the same to him.

Varity watched on as the friends bid each other farewell. At that moment, and for the first time, she finally saw the real Arabelle. Long accustomed to feeling threatened by her beauty and irked by her friendship with Madlyn, Varity now saw the woman before her as compassionate, protective, and fiercely independent. A captivating spectacle to the eyes, a gentle companion to the soul, and genuinely authentic in every way.

"Will you be okay?" Varity asked Arabelle, her voice carrying a touch of regret.

Arabelle turned and smiled warmly at Varity, a smile full of forgiveness and reassurance. "Always," she replied. "And you?"

Varity smiled back. "Believe it or not, I'm going to join those two."

Arabelle cocked her head in curiosity. "Really? That's an interesting choice."

"Yeah, why not? I figured I could procreate with one, and break the heart of the other," Varity laughed.

Arabelle chuckled. "Interesting decision. Which will be which?"

"A lady never tells; guess you'll have to join us to find out," Varity grinned. "Come with us,"

Arabelle's eyes flashed with indecision as she replayed the tempting words in her mind. The notion of a self-imposed exile felt like a risky leap into the unknown. Yet, an unspoken understanding tugged at her. She knew this would be the best way.

Arabelle had her own reasons, known exclusively to her. Safeguarding a special project in her future was paramount, requiring protection from external influences. "I can't," she replied.

Varity nodded. If she knew one thing about Arabelle, it was that she wouldn't change her mind.

As the trio walked away in the distance, Arabelle felt an overwhelming desire to join them and become an essential part of the group of friends she had always known, a bond she might have taken for granted. The magnetic pull of camaraderie enticed her, urging her to abandon the solitary path she often walked.

Yet, despite the powerful longing, Arabelle's legs felt rigid, as if held back by an unseen force. A conflict arose within her—a profound yearning for belonging clashed with the fierce independence that defined her spirit. The scars of past heartaches whispered caution in her ears, reminding her of the fragility of love and the pain of potential loss.

She watched them leaving without shedding a tear, a stoic figure masking the complex emotions churning within.

As their laughter faded, Arabelle stood alone, resolute, but there was one last thing she wanted to do before she said goodbye to her old life forever.

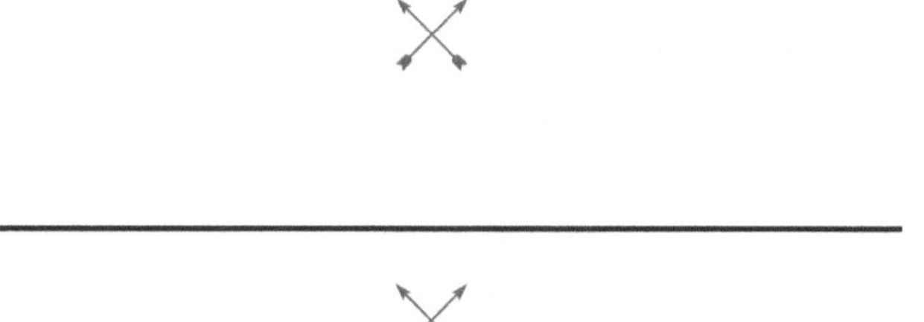

IN THE DIM LIGHT OF the half-burnt cabin, Arabelle moved with a quiet urgency, her eyes scanning the familiar kitchen. The wooden shelves, once lined with everyday items, now served as a treasure trove for her impending journey into the wild. Her face was a picture of determination as she reached for a set of lightweight pots, swiftly stowing them in her worn backpack.

Cans of beans and neatly packed dried fruits joined the ensemble, promising sustenance in the heart of nature. Her fingers deftly grabbed a large tin of hot chocolate, a small luxury she refused to leave behind. As the setting sun cast a soft glow through the cabin window, she secured reusable water bottles, their emptiness a promise to be filled from the untouched streams of the wilderness.

After gathering all she could carry, she paused and took stock of her surroundings. She expected that revisiting Madlyn's cottage would bring her pain, yet somehow, being surrounded by her belongings proved to be a source of comfort. Despite the frustrating disarray of Madlyn's house, the mess she used to hate, Arabelle now felt like she was home.

The miniature sculptures, made from salvaged scrap metal, shards of glass, and discarded electronics, hinted at the beauty that could be found amidst destruction.

Memories flooded Arabelles mind, triggered by each piece of furniture and every trinket. Each item held a reminder, encapsulating a story of friendship and a chapter of love.

Amid the artifacts, a few carefully preserved photographs offered a glimpse into the past. Faded images depicted scenes of life before the upheaval, capturing moments of joy, love, and normalcy.

Each photograph carried a bittersweet weight, evoking a sense of nostalgia for a time that could never be reclaimed. Arabelle carefully picked up each photo, placing them one by one into a neat pile before sliding them delicately into her backpack pocket. The once seeming clutter had transformed into cherished keepsakes, making her realise the purpose behind Madlyn's decision to keep useless items. Everything served as a poignant reminder of the most beautiful moments in her life.

Arabelle's eyes, blurred from tears, stopped on the safe. She shook her head in frustration as she recalled dragging the gift from the town, cursing and swearing at its weight. So determined to deliver it to Madlyn. Madlyn, with her secret diaries and important papers, she knew she would end up loving it, if not first to protest its randomness.

Arabelle wiped her eyes to focus better on the present that had given her shoulder pain for two weeks. The weighty safe door stood ajar, revealing papers and books haphazardly piled in a typically Madlyn way. Arabelle paused., she now had entry into the secret thoughts that Madlyn had once guarded so dearly.

Her mind raced; a rapid-fire of thoughts and worries flooding her consciousness.

Her head respected privacy, but her heart yearned for the words within.

She stepped away, then hesitated, halting in a moment of confusion.

The words would reconnect her once more; Madlyn would understand. They had shared everything. Reading her diary wouldn't be a breach of privacy but a tribute to her memory.

She stepped back. She could leave without connecting with her friend once more.

Arabelle pulled open the safe door and dropped to her knees. Just holding the book felt like a blessing, and she found comfort in its presence.

She casually flipped through the pages until her eyes landed on a spot seemingly handpicked by fate.

Arabelle began to read.

LAST NIGHT I COULDN'T sleep.

Betraying my whole kin sits unpleasantly in my mind at times, but then I watch them, and I'm reminded of the meaningless life they all lead. They are fodder, they are waiting around to be food. Surviving on scraps and fear, I can't do this anymore. I can't let kindness destroy my destiny.

I will be strong; I will live for decades after they are all gone, and I will finally step out of Belle's shadow. I will be the perfect one, the fighter, the hero. I will protect and not have to be protected. Imagine that feeling!

AS THE WORDS REVEALED themselves, Arabelle's face registered a mix of shock and disbelief. With wide-eyed astonishment, she repeatedly scanned the sentences, as if grappling with the implausibility of the information presented.

MORRISON, YOU STUPID bastard, you will pay for this, trying to save the world with your vaccine. Save who? You don't save us, you make us all weak, make us all Bot food. Destroy my dream and I will destroy yours. I will destroy you. I will destroy everyone if it means I will become better than this frail body that holds me.

Love is a liability, friendship is a straitjacket, this Kin, these people, they are an anchor around my legs. Dragging me to the bottom of the ocean. I will not drown. I will not go down with this sinking ship.

THE ROOM SUDDENLY FELT very small, a cocoon of confined space tightening around, as if the walls whispered secrets too intimate for the expanse they contained. Arabelle felt a sudden surge of vomit fill her throat. Her entire body was covered in a clammy sheen. The air was thick, almost suffocating. As she turned the page, her trembling fingers struggled to lift the weight of the words written on the last entry.

FUCK YOU URONGA, YOU get what you accept, and I no longer accept being human. I no longer accept my Kinship. Hemoes ruled the world, and I want to rule the world.

Chapter Thirty-Five

BARRY, THE BIOBOT, sat quietly in Dr. Stanley Cryton's bedroom, awaiting his final breath. Despite his hunger, draining his father's blood before his death seemed excessively cruel.

He tapped his metal fingers impatiently on the arm of the chair as he waited.

Brain Biorhythms present. Pulse rate is one twenty.

It had been days. His steel legs bounced furiously, like a junkie waiting for a fix.

Blood pressure is ninety over seventy.

His agitated photoreceptive eyes flicked restlessly from one corner of the room to the other.

Body temperature is thirty-five degrees.

Barry rose to his feet with a deliberate slowness, thoughtfully approaching the death bed.

Breathing shallow. Consciousness is present.

The old man opened his eyes, gazing lovingly at his lifelong companion. "Barry, are you bloody good?" he asked sheepishly.

The BioBot smiled sweetly at his creator, and without a word lifted the doctor's skinny pale arm, using the tip of his steel finger to slice through the radial vein.

"Barry... No... Stop."

The BioBot smiled reassuringly as his steel hand opened, revealing a concealed vacuum-like machine within. He gently placed his hand over the old man's wrist wound and applied pressure.

The final sound to reach Dr. Stanley Cryton's ears was a soft gentle sucking noise.

Born into a military family in rural Queensland, Second Lieutenant Benjamin Daley's journey began with a deep-rooted sense of duty. Excelling in academics and sports, he chose the Australian Defence Force Academy, blending learning with military training.

Commissioned as an officer, Daley quickly stood out for his strategic acumen and decisive leadership. Recognised for his potential, he underwent specialised training in intelligence and reconnaissance. Deployed on a peacekeeping mission during the Third Ward, he faced diplomatic challenges while ensuring his team's safety.

Through these experiences, Daley earned a reputation for adaptability and unwavering commitment. His peers felt he was a rising star, poised to shape the future of the Australian Army.

Benjamin's sacrifice went unnoticed in the world's recovery from the war, receiving only a subdued acknowledgment. There were no grand celebrations or radiant tributes; instead, his name lingered in the margins of history, a mere whisper amidst more monumental tales. Words like "served his country" and "ultimate sacrifice" felt inadequate, unable to capture the profound ordeal etched into every fibre of Benjamin's being.

His story wasn't just one of sacrifice; it unfolded in the unrelenting rhythm of hunger and pain, each moment a testament to his endurance. Each page of his experience turned with excruciating slowness, as if time itself was reluctant to reveal his story, a story that surpassed words.

Following Benjamin's act, the Nanoquarks emerged victorious, skilfully orchestrating unintentional chaos. Their metal-eating prowess wrought havoc on the machinery that once fuelled the heartbeat of manufacturing. The aftermath revealed a transformed landscape, where BioBots—a symbol of organised efficiency—wandered in disarray.

Hunger painted their every movement with a sense of desperate urgency as they scavenged through their once-coordinated assembly, now scattered. Deprived of their former vitality, they stood as silent echoes from a bygone era that eloquently illustrated the fragility of memory. Some lingered, wandering aimlessly, with hunger gnawing away at their existence. They became mere remnants, weak, starving empty vessels. Ghosts from New Zealand's history.

Restless and uneasy, Shyla sat on the edge of Quillian's imposing office chair, her every movement displaying her discomfort. Quick, brief glances toward the sturdy wooden door revealed her anticipation, and lines of anxiety etched across her face as she awaited Quillian's predictable entrance. An entrance that would never come.

The room seemed to hold its breath, anticipating the storm that would accompany his presence. The silence, devoid of his deep, smooth voice and authoritative footsteps, rung with palpable tension, heightening Shyla's discomfort.

Across the room, Roland fidgeted nervously, his eyes darting between the door and Shyla. His presence, typically unnoticed in the background, now carried a certain weight, mirroring Shyla's sense of anticipation. The air felt charged, thick with unspoken expectations of an impending confrontation. She was now the boss, but by what authority?

Outside Quillian's office, a different saga unfolded. The once-mighty Hemovitalists, rulers of a now crumbling realm, clung to a semblance of life in the shadows of their former glory. No longer puppeteers of their dominion, they existed in isolation, survival reliant on the dwindling numbers of human volunteers providing reluctant sustenance. The once-indomitable reign had transformed into a tale of humility, the Hemovitalists humbled by their altered fate and weakened by a relentless adversity.

In their new found pursuit of mere survival, grand ambitions that once fuelled them were now a distant memory.

Their story had unfolded like the pages of an epic novel, revealing power dynamics and survival strategies overriding their diminished role. The quiet desperation of the Hemovitalists seemed to resonate through every action, vividly depicting their struggle to navigate a world no longer bowing to their command. As the years went by, the branches of their reign would gradually wither away, and during this time, the walls of Quillian's office would bear witness to Shyla's quiet defiance and Roland's uneasy complicity. Both of them, in their own unique ways, would come to represent the larger drama unfolding outside the boundaries of that room as the Hemovitalist struggle to accept their fate.

Among the vast emptiness of the new world, moments of human presence emerged like fleeting apparitions. The once-thriving species, now reduced to a rare existence, navigating the ruins of their former lives. Each human figure seemed to be a solitary wanderer, a lone echo in the vast silence that enveloped the landscape.

Humans had become the rarest of species. The whispers of these large hidden kinships, which were once seen as a guiding light for humanity amidst the threat of extinction, ultimately proved to be nothing but mere stories. Hopes pinned on these murmurs of communal strength shattered like fragile glass, leaving behind a stark reality of isolation. The imagined alliances between neighbours dissipated into the winds of despair sweeping through the remnants of human civilization.

Amidst the ruins of shattered aspirations and broken dreams, a separation unfolded among the survivors, adding a new level of uncertainty. Some stubbornly clung to the belief in the possibility of reclaiming dominance, their ambitions echoing through time like a distant anthem of resilience. With their eyes fixed on the horizon, these people carried the weight of a heritage that once placed humanity at the pinnacle of the natural world.

While others, others among the remnants of the species, found comfort in the acceptance of a different narrative. Contentment became their refuge, not in surrender, but in the embrace of a newfound role. They no longer desired to rule over a world that had been tarnished by the wounds of war; instead, they embraced a humble role as mere elements of the very environment they had once aimed to dominate. Their eyes were not focused on a lost throne but on the intricate web of life that emerged after their species' near-extinction.

Once a symbol of the ruling species' ambitions, the landscape now painted a picture of survival and resilience—a testament to the unwavering spirit of a species determined to write its own story. Humanity humbly embraced a new role, realizing its position as a mere thread in the intricate tapestry of the world.

The world was the only victor in this war. Unburdened of humanity and its creations, Mother nature silently took charge, initiated a silent reclamation, nurturing the world back to a balanced existence.

As the first rays of the new dawn illuminated the battered earth, shoots of resilient cautiously emerged from scorched soil. Each tender sprout symbolised renewal, showcasing the natural world's unstoppable spirit. The once-thick air, tainted by the acrid scent of conflict, transformed into a gentle whisper of leaves and the subtle hum of insects reclaiming their territory.

Nature's healing touch extended beyond visible scars on the land. Birds melodiously trilled, cautiously returning to their once-abandoned nests. Meandering streams, once polluted by BioBot creation, sparkled with renewed vitality as they carved through the healing terrain. Flora, once trampled by warfare, stood tall in a display of fertile defiance.

As it had done for millennia after millennia, the earth underwent a transformation, a rebirth that surpassed the scars of conflict. Human engineered relics, overgrown with vines and foliage, became leftovers of a bygone era, swallowed by nature, reclaiming its dominion.

The rhythmic rainfall on the rejuvenated soil created a symphony of sound that celebrated the resurgence. Once held back by human ambitions, nature burst forth in a grand display of renewal, overwhelming the senses with its sights, sounds, and scents. The liberated world painted a portrait of balance, war scars transformed into a testament of resilience.

As seasons cycled through their eternal ballet, the world carried the memory of conflict in whispers and rustling—a poignant reminder of nature's transformative power. In this peaceful symphony of renewal, the Earth materialised as a vibrant testament to the continuous patterns of growth and decay, reminiscent of a Phoenix's ascent from the ashes, tenacious and unconstrained.

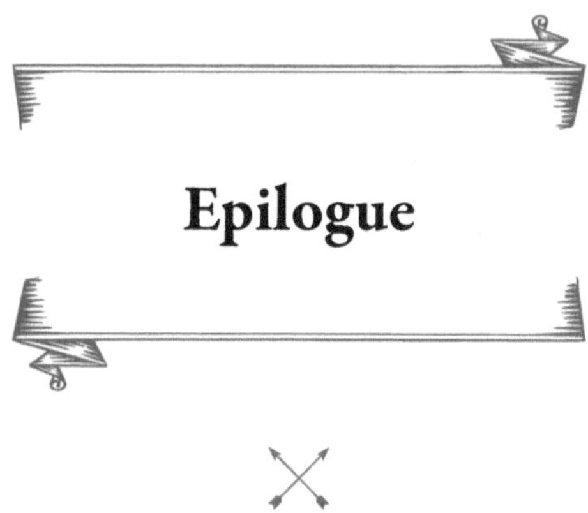

Epilogue

NESTLED HIGH IN THE imposing snow-covered mountains of the southern Alps, a cozy cabin stood as a sanctuary against the wintry embrace of nature. The landscape, blanketed in untouched white snow, glistened under the soft glow of the winter sun. The cabin's timber walls, adorned with hanging plants, harmonised with the frosted trees that surrounded it.

Smoke spiralled from the chimney, a reassuring sign of warmth and comfort within. The world outside was hushed and serene, offering a breathtaking backdrop of tranquillity and wonder to a world no longer at war.

Arabelle set the steaming cup of hot chocolate carefully upon the table, then settled into her chair in serene contemplation. She had reached a point of tranquillity in her journey, leaving behind tumultuous battles, the painful loss of dear friends, and a tragic love that was once forbidden but now forgotten. These experiences now resided in the realm of memories, haunting her only during the night, where they danced through her mind as she slept.

She gently pushed her hand across her stomach. Sensing the normally hard, flat surface now hugely swollen and taut beneath her touch. Arabelle made no attempt to hide her smile. A proud grin took over her face almost instantly. She could feel the life inside her and her changing body made for an even stronger connection. The thought of the potential consequences of a Human-Hemo hybrid didn't cross her mind. In that very moment, an intense maternal tenderness that coursed through her heart with every beat that nourished her child consumed her.

Arabelle knew her child would be a unique and remarkable being, the first of its kind. The baby's human lineage would grant them humility and the capacity to generate their own blood. Their Hemovitalists heritage would bestow upon them exceptional strength and rejuvenation.

Choosing a name for her daughter, Arabelle settled on Mirai, a Japanese name that meant 'Hope for the Future.'

Mirai became the best of humankind, the Alpha and the Omega. A visionary with determination, courage, and an unwavering commitment to progress and empowerment for all. Her very existence united and healed a fractured world.

In Arabelle's Seventy-Seventh year of life, two years before her death, she witnessed her daughter being crowned the first Queen of the new age.

Under Queen Mirai's reign, the world found solace and rejuvenation, infused with the hope that her name had always promised.

| Page

About the Author

Claire Rye's self-assessment as an "old-school head banging, vegetarian, nature loving, history fan and sci-fi geek" captures the eclectic nature of her interests and influences.Understandably, her self-published novels are diverse in genres. Ranging from fantasy, science fiction, mystery to erotica.Claire's non-conformist writing style means each book is unpredictable. However, regardless of the category of story, the quirky yet relatable characters and surprising revelations make for a rewarding journey.Claire Rye started to explore the world of writing in 2015 when her flair for the written word was discovered accidentally. She kept an informal blog while travelling through the United States and Europe. Claire found that her love of the unconventional helped her to look beyond the superficial. She discovered the ability to see 'the story behind the story' of the people and places she encountered.An overwhelmingly positive and excited response to her travel blog triggered a curiosity that lead to an expansion of her story telling.Claire Rye was born in Sydney Australia and currently lives on the Gold Coast. She continues to travel and develop her writing skills. You can find out more about Claire Rye and her works at www.clairerye.net

Read more at www.clairerye.net.